The Remembrance Album of Harriet Pruden

ISBN: 978-1-60910-033-9

This is a work of historical fiction, though the vast majority of the people and all of the poems are real. The narrative and incidents are the author's conjecture based on his interpretation of the poems and on extensive research into the available history of the people involved.

Cover photo: the remnants of the embroidered bouquet on the cover of Harriet's album.

Printed in the United States of America.

www.rkpate.com

Booklocker.com, Inc. 2009

The Remembrance Album of Harriet Pruden

The 175 year reunion of the seventy people who composed and compiled their verses for Harriet's album

Based on a true story

RICHARD K. PATE

Dedicated to the many, many people who
had a hand in the making of Harriet's album.

Acknowledgement

Many thanks to the staff at the Athens County Historical Society & Museum, especially Cheryl Dorr Wright. Thanks also to Diana Zornow at the Elkhart County Historical Museum for all her help. Jeanette Berard, Research Librarian at the Thousand Oaks Library System, was indispensable. Thanks to Paul Pruden, Gerald Smith and Sue Sullivan for providing invaluable supplemental information. Thanks to all my editors! Special thanks to JLS. Terry Ehret, I still owe you a dinner.

To the many professors who were nice enough to respond to my inquiries, you were all so gracious and helpful, thank you.

Author's Note

The poems are presented here in three chapters in chronological order. They were entered randomly in the original album.

If the poet did not identify himself or herself they are noted as 'anonymous.' Liberty was taken to allow important people in the story to have a say by assigning them a poem if they did not make a contribution or did not sign their piece. Assigned poems are not signed and are noted as 'anonymous' at the index. The exceptions are Martha A. Light's poems. None of her poems were signed but were identified by her handwriting and by the similar subject matter.

The spelling, grammar and punctuation in the work from the nineteenth century is as it appears in the original album. Any corrections appear italicized in parenthesis and are provided for clarity.

Table of Contents

Introduction

The following collection of poetry was found hand-written by multiple authors in a single volume dating from 1831 to 1909. The poems chronicle events in one American settler family's history and tell a poignant and surprisingly personal true story. The accompanying narrative, supplied by the author, is based on research of the poems, the persons involved, and the towns and times in which they lived. It is largely factual and otherwise faithful to natural inferences.

The album begins as an intervention by a well-to-do family to persuade their daughter, Harriet, the town sweetheart, to give up her reckless dream of pioneering on the Western Frontier. From there the book takes on a life of its own as it makes its way westward, each writer adding their own voice to this story of determination, adventure, hardship, and love.

Chapter One

Athens, Ohio - 1831 to 1836

A.G. Brown: My name is Archibald Green Brown. I was born the same year my family moved to Ohio, 1798. There was no Athens or Ohio University in those days, just some scattered settlers' cabins, one of which was ours. The site on which Ohio University sits had been, just a few years before, the favorite hunting ground of the local Indians (most of the Indian wars in Ohio were over by the early 1800's, though it was not until 1818 that the Miami tribe gave up their last piece of ground). In 1830, when this story begins, there were only twenty-four states in the Union, with a total population of thirteen million, less than a million in Ohio. Andrew Jackson, 'Old Hickory,' was two years into his Presidency. I had graduated from Ohio University and was then studying law, was the County Recorder, had founded and run Athens' very first newspaper, *The Athens Mirror,* and was acting Justice of the Peace.

I remember well Miss Harriet and the circumstances surrounding the creation of her commonplace book. It was in 1831 that I was asked to be the master-reader for the compilation of Harriet's book. I was busy in those days and would never have agreed to teach private lessons on poetry had it not been for Harriet Pruden. She was the most enchanting young lady in Athens back then. Not only was she exceedingly beautiful, she was also most kind and considerate.

Harriet was the daughter of a prominent Athens family and was sixteen years old in 1831. She talked constantly of visiting the Wild West, seeing the fierce Indians and exploring the boundless open space. Harriet had the 'wanderlust.'

Mrs. Mary Pruden approached me with the idea of creating a commonplace book for her daughter. It was to be in the form of a keepsake or remembrance album, with the purpose of convincing Harriet to stay in Athens. Harriet had fallen in love with a young carpenter, one Emanuel Light. He was working in Athens but was from Logan, some thirty miles north of Athens. Unlike Harriet, Emanuel was not well-to-do and like many poorer people of the time, intended to head west to become a settler and claim some of the new lands waiting to be tamed. Harriet, at that tender age, had announced that she would marry Emanuel and accompany him into the vast West. This created quite a stir in Athens. Truly she had no idea of the hardship and toil associated with a settler's life. She envisioned living in the Far West as an exciting adventure. At one point she confessed to me that though she loved her family, she had no intention of complying with her parents' plans for her. Her intention was not to marry a rich gentleman and live in the East. She found the whole idea boring and limiting. No, she wanted adventure and excitement. She wanted to be a part of the country's "Westward Expansion." Lewis and Clark were her heroes and embodied her own dreams. She and Emanuel wanted to follow in their footsteps.

Virtually everyone in Athens felt Harriet was making a huge mistake. She was young and innocent and Emanuel was like Odysseus' syren, as he was leading her into harm's way. We all talked with her and tried to convince her it was just a passing infatuation. Life in the Far West as a settler was for people who had no choice but to head to the territories. Harriet would politely listen but would not give up her dream. Once it became clear that the talking was going nowhere, Mary Pruden came up with the idea of creating the Remembrance Album for her daughter. She felt that perhaps a concerted effort by all her friends and family would show Harriet just how loved she was and might convince her to change her mind. If it did not work, then at least she would have the book to remember everyone by. Sentimental poetry was very popular in those days and Harriet was a great fan of verse, hence the format for her book. Because of my fondness for Harriet and knowledge of the tradition of commonplace books, I agreed to participate in the project. I insisted that Harriet's commonplace book be based upon classical examples which date back to the Renaissance. The poetry, often in the form of apothegms, would strive to teach the reader (Harriet) important, time-honored truths about the world. It would be compiled as a communal act and would be led by a master-reader who would lead the group to correct understanding of texts. Further, I hoped that Harriet would pass the book down to succeeding generations of her family as many older commonplace books had been.

The class was formed and we met weekly for a few months to compose the poetry and begin the album. We read the pieces aloud and refined them. I checked them for spelling and punctuation and recommended books from the shelves of the University library for the students to use for reference. We had a grand time.

Harriet was overwhelmed by her gift. So much so that we thought we had actually convinced her to stay in Athens. Ultimately the young couple would leave, but the commonplace book did give Harriet pause. It delayed their departure for quite some time. Towards the end of 1836, the young couple finally eloped.

It was my honor to write the first entry in the album. I chose a quote from Pollok's *Course of Time* as it subtly conveyed my own feelings that Harriet and Emanuel should be together. I hoped that the couple would stay in Athens and be married. I liked Emanuel and hoped he would eventually be accepted by the Pruden family. He would then not need to take our Harriet away. Of course, I could not say this directly, being in the minority. Most people wanted nothing to do with young Mr. Light, especially Harriet's mother.

Virtue
From Pollok's "Course of Time"

"For as by nature, sin is dark and loves
The dark, still hiding from himself in gloom
And in the darkness hell is still itself
The darker hell, and the severest ever
When all is wo, so virtue, ever fair!
Doth by a sympathy as strong as binds
Two equal hearts, well plowed in wedded love
Forever seek the light, forever seek
All fair and lovely things, all beauteous forms,
All images of excellence and truth;
And from her own essential being pure
As flows the fount of life that spirits drink,
Doth to herself give light, ner from her beams
As native as her own existence
Can be divorced, nor of her glory shorn."

A.G. Brown, Athens, Ohio Jan 25, 1831

(AG Brown married Priscilla K. Crippen January 8, 1824. They had no children.)

♦ ♦ ♦ ♦

Mary Pruden: I was at my wits end. We had tried everything to convince Harriet that this infatuation of hers was just that, an infatuation! Of all Harriet's suitors why she chose that carpenter, was beyond me. He was a nice enough boy but he had little promise in my eyes. He would never be able to care for Harriet in the style to which she was accustomed. Moreover, he was leading her into harm's way and was seriously threatening her purity. Up until then she had been such a joy, always happy, pious and compassionate. My husband Silas and I raised all our children to judge others by their character. We taught them to treat all good people with respect regardless of their station in life. That did not mean we wanted or expected Harriet to become involved with a person from such a different social standing.

There were many young men in Athens with great promise whom Harriet could have had, but they all lacked the desire to wander off into the opening West, and thus they were all rejected by my daughter. She would say, "Mother your own parents were pioneer settlers right here in Athens as were you and Father. Why would you deny me my chance?" My Father, Alvin Bingham (known by most as Old Judge Bingham) and my mother moved here around 1800, so Harriet was right. That only increased the fear I felt for her. She did not understand the dangers on the frontier.

As part of America's newly emerging middle class, my husband and I adhered to the tenets of The Cult of Domesticity of True Womanhood. It taught that women like Harriet were weak and delicate and belonged safe at home, not gallivanting around in the wilderness. Settling the new westerly lands was for others, not for the Prudens –especially not for the Pruden womenfolk. After all my praying and crying and arguing, she would not be deterred. It was late in 1830 when it became clear to all of Athens that Harriet was determined to venture west. Shortly after she announced that she would leave us was when I decided to create her Remembrance Album. I hoped it would have the effect of changing Harriet's mind and bringing her to her senses. It worked, for a while. The great number of people who wrote verses to her touched us all deeply. She was truly Athens' favorite daughter and it shows in the absolutely heartfelt verses written to her. As I had hoped, the album became a tangible reality that reminded Harriet of what I constantly told her: friends are the most important thing in life. She would never find as many true and dedicated friends as she already had at home. The album drove that point home. She stayed with us an additional six years.

Mr. Light was from Logan, over the hills, and so was not always in Athens but did often find work here. There were good stretches of time when he was away. I did my best to get her interested in other potential husbands during those times. You surely cannot blame me for trying.

I purchased the blank album at Judge Currier's mercantile after Christmas in 1830 and embroidered a beautiful bouquet of daisies on the regal purple covering. My daughter, Rebecca, and I organized the friends and family who would participate. It was agreed to in advance that we, as a group, would try to dissuade Harriet from her chosen course by demonstrating our collective love for her and by sending messages in our poetry, expressing our concern for her well-being. We managed to keep the class and book a secret from Harriet. We presented it to her, as I recall, in April of 1831. It had only a few poems in it at the time; many of the students continued to work on their pieces. They would later enter their poems while socializing at our home during the many parties and gatherings. The album was left on a table in the foyer for that purpose.

Professor Brown did such a good job of being master-reader and overseeing the album's creation. The few months of classes were a joy to all concerned. Each session was a delight to attend and the outcome was most pleasing. We sometimes met at the library at the University which was quite a treat for the girls and ladies in the class. Women were not admitted to any university in those days.

Archibald, Professor Brown that is, thought I had missed the hidden message of his entry. He said that it was a warning to Harriet to protect her virtue when in actuality it was a sympathetic voice to Harriet and *him*. It was not that hard to discern, considering especially the use of the phrase, "wedded love." Needless to say I was not pleased with his entry. We were, after all, trying to keep Harriet's mind off getting married to young Mr. Light. However, Harriet and Professor Brown were close friends and I knew he sympathized with her. In the end I knew it was all in the Creator's hands and beyond my power to influence.

May cloudless beams of grace and truth
Adorn my daughter's ope'ning youth;
Long happy in her native home,
Among it's fragrant groves to roam,
May choicest blessings her attend

In Parents Brothers Sisters Friends;
May no rude wish asail her breast
To love this world by all confest
Is only given us to prepare
For one eternal bright and fair
This world shall then no force retain
It's syren's voice shall charm in vain
Religion's, aid true, peace will bring,
Her voice with joy shall praises sing
To him whose streams of mercy flow
To cheer the heart oer charged with woe
And whilst retirements sweets we know
Forever praise redeeming love

Mary Pruden

(Of Mary's twelve children seven died before she did in or around 1838. Is it any wonder she wanted Harriet to stay at home?)

♦ ♦ ♦ ♦

Mary Perkins: I am Mrs. John Perkins. My father-in-law, Dr. Eliphas Perkins, had one of the first log cabins in Athens. That was back around 1800, along with the Bingham's and Currier's. So yes, we are one of Athens' founding families. Athens is the second oldest town in Ohio. The Miami and other Ohio Indians had mainly surrendered the state and moved west after the Battle of Fallen Timbers in 1794. This left the land ready to be claimed and claim it we did.

Many years later, when we began this album, we were settled and prospering. In 1831 Athens was twenty-seven years old, and considered a small town in the West, but was working hard to be more than a fledgling community. There was no need for Harriet to venture forth as her elder generation had. In those days a proper young woman was supposed to concern herself only with piety, purity, domesticity, and submissiveness. Such were the times.

I was happy to contribute a poem to Harriet's album. First, being a close and personal friend of Silas and Mary's I wanted to do my part. Second, I felt, once upon a time, I had been Harriet. That is to say, when I was sixteen I also was a beauty. In those days I little understood that life was not just a continual merry time of adventure and love. Now I know better, having learned the hard way. Having babies continuously for a dozen years will do that to one. I missed my gay years of youth but my experiences have taught me to rely on my faith in the hereafter, and if "true wisdom" is "early sought and gained," then those certainties "in age will give thee rest," which is all we can ask. That was my message to Harriet.

Harriet was an uncommon beauty and had a fine character and poise. She was the epitome of grace, as had I been in my day. Moreover she was without prejudice and she made friends with people from all walks of life. Harriet believed in the spirit of freedom and in fighting for what is right. She was very interested in the Underground Railroad, the fight good-hearted people were waging to help runaway slaves get to Canada or free states like Ohio.

"Now in the morn of life, when youth
With vital ardour glows
And shines in all the fairest charms
That beauty can disclose.
Deep in thy soul, before its powers
Are yet by vice enslaved,
Be thy Creator's glorious name
And character engraved;
Ere yet the shades of sorrow cloud
The sunshine of thy days;
And cares and toils, in countless round,
Encompass all thy ways:
Ere yet thy heart the woes of age,
With vain regret, deplore,
And sadly muse on former joys
That now return no more.

True wisdom early sought and gain'd,
In age will give thee rest,
O then, improve the morn of life,
To make its coming blest!"

Mary Perkins Feb 21, 1831

♦ ♦ ♦ ♦

Adeline L. Currier: I also am a member of one of Athens oldest families. My father, Judge Ebenezer Currier, came to Athens in 1806. He is known as one of Athens' pioneer merchants. My family and Harriet's were good friends and often socialized. Harriet and I were fond of collecting the latest poetry. We would gather it from books, newspapers and magazines. We were also fond of pestering Professor Brown to loan us the latest books he collected for his own personal library.

I must say I did not approve of Emanuel Light. He and Harriet met in the winter of 1830 and fell in love. He was then a carpenter from Logan, Ohio, his family was originally from Virginia, and he was taking my good friend away from me. Somehow he convinced poor Harriet to go with him to the wilds of Northern Indiana and become a settler! Northern Indiana was well named; the natives were heavily armed and everywhere. There were Potowatomi, Ottawa and Chippewa (or Objibwa), and they considered themselves one people. In 1762, under Pontiac, they had captured ten of thirteen British forts. The Potowatomi had conducted the Fort Dearborn Massacre in 1812. The destroyed fort had been in the small settlement of Chicago, very close to where Mr. Light intended to take my friend.

I tried to convince her not to go, it was inviting certain doom. Harriet was, in 1831, a fresh green leaf with so much promise. She was in the spring of her life and was an idealist and optimist and not afraid to chase down her dreams. This, in a time when we middle class women were not allowed to have dreams of our own. This poem was written to try and show her that nothing lasts forever, especially some fragile thing like her or a leaf. We were taught to be prepared for sorrow and misery because of life's uncertainties. To minimize uncertainties, remaining in a secure environment was only prudent and wise. Women like Harriet were most definitely not supposed to become adventurers; it was socially unacceptable. The rough life outside the home of the middle class was the man's domain only in those days; all the women's journals of the day said so.

I found it ironic that even the class formed to create this album (which I mention in my poem) paralleled life's fleeting nature. It remains one of my favorite memories because of the great pride and pleasure we all took in meeting, composing and compiling our poetry to Harriet. It was over so quickly; like all earthly pleasures it lasted but a short time.

The Leaf

It came with springs soft sun and showers
Mid bursting buds and bursting flowers.
It flourished on the same light stem,
It drank the same clear dew with them
The crimson tints of summer morn
That gilded one, did each adorn.
The breeze that whispered light and brief
To bud and blossom kiss'd the leaf,
When o'er the leaf the tempest flew,
The bud and blossom trembled too.
But its companions passed away,
And left the leaf to lone decay,
The gentle gales of spring went by,
The fruits and flowers of summer die,
The autumn winds swept o'er the hill;
And winters breath came cold and chill.
The leaf now yielded to the blast,
And on the rushing stream was cast,
Far far it glided on the sea
And whirled and eddied wearily,
Till suddenly it sunk to rest,

And slumbered on the ocean's breast.
Thus life begins its morning hour,
Bright as the birthday of the flower -
Thus passes like leaves away,
As withered and lost us as they.
Beneath the present roof we meet
In joyous groups and gaily greet
The golden beams of love and light,
That kindle to the youthful sight,
But soon we part and one by one,
Like leaves and flowers, the group is done.
One gentle spirit seeks the tomb,
His brow yet fresh with childhood's bloom.
Another treads the path of fame,
And barters peace to win a name,
Another still tempts fortunes wave,
And seeking wealth, secures a grave
The last grasps yet the brittle thread -
Though friends are gone and joy is dead,
Still dare the dark and fretful tide,
And clutches at its power and pride
Till suddenly the waters sever,
And like the leaf he sinks forever

Transcribed by your friend
Adeline L. Currier
Athens 3rd Mo. 17th 1831

♦ ♦ ♦ ♦

A.L.C.: Yes, it is me again, Adeline Currier. This is the second poem I wrote to Harriet back on March 17th in 1831. I did not author this piece however. It was written by John Gardiner Calkins Brainard and was just published when I entered it into Harriet's album. In the old album this poem follows Martha Light's poem, *The Cloud* (see page 109), but mine was written some forty years before. We definitely had different opinions about clouds! As I previously mentioned, in my day we sought stability and certainty as they promised security. A cloud, being transient and ever-changing was not a symbol of security. Where Harriet was going was so uncertain and dangerous, well, you can understand why we were concerned for her. I hoped this poem would bring her some comfort in the wilderness.

A Fragment

"Yon cloud, 'tis bright and beautiful - it floats
Alone in God's horizon - on its edge
The stars seem hung like pearls - it looks as pure
As 'twere an angels shroud - the white cymar
Of purity just peeping through its folds,
To give a pitying look on this sad world
Go visit it, and find that all is false,
Its glories are but fog - and its white form
Is plighted to some coming thunderquest.
The rain, the wind, the lightning have their source
In such bright meetings. Gaze not on the clouds
However beautiful - gaze at the sky,
The clear, blue, tranquil, fix'd and glorious sky."

A.L.C.......Athens March 17th 1831

(Adeline was born November 2, 1813 in Athens County. She married Oscar W. Brown in 1833 and died March 3, 1893)

♦ ♦ ♦ ♦

Iounne Brown: Frankly, Harriet was too attractive for her own good. Men were drawn to her like moths to a flame. I felt once she had matured a bit she would forget this foolishness about becoming a pioneer and settle down in Ohio. However, in 1831 she was a wide-eyed beauty and as such was distracted by love and youthful ideas. She envisioned a grand adventure with a gala ending where she and her beau would live happily ever after, seldom a reality for settlers. She was quite the romantic in those days. I chose this poem for Harriet's album to remind her of a time-honored truth.

Sympathy

How lovely is yon star of night,
That shines amid the shades of even,
And revels in its pearly light,
The brightest, purest gem of heaven;
But brighter far, the tearful eye,
That wakes and weeps at misery's sigh
How sweet the flower's at early dawn,
When first they meet the orienst beam,
Glist'ning amid the dews of morn,
Like sun-rays brightning on the stream
Yet sweeter far, the friendly voice,
That bids the heart rejoice.

Iounne Brown Athens, March 28th 1831

♦ ♦ ♦ ♦

S ..... B .....: I am the eldest son of Silas Pruden and the only offspring from his first marriage with my mother, Rebecca Carmichael. My name is Samuel Baldwin Pruden. I was born January 17, 1798 in Morristown, New Jersey. In 1831 Harriet was an enchanting, spirited young woman with all the idealism of youth. Life had not yet had the chance to beat her down. She had yet to discover its oh-so-fleeting nature. I begin my poem with the famous quote addressed to virgins by Robert Herrick (1591-1674), to make the most of their youthful years, those days and that happiness does not last long. I wanted to show sympathy with Harriet, but instead warned her that the idealism of youth quickly fades.

Youth

"gather the rosebuds while ye may
old time is still a flying;
and that same flower that blooms today
tomorrow shall be dying."

"What are all thy boasted tomorrows?
Tender sorrows, transient pleasures,
Anxious hopes and jealous fears,
Laughing hours, and mourning years
Deck'd with brightest tints at morn,
At twilight with'ring on a thorn,
Like the gentle rose of spring,
Chill'd by every zephyr's wings;
Ah! How soon its colour flies,
Blushes, trembles, falls, and dies
What is youth? A smiling sorrow
Blithe to-day and sad tomorrow;
Never fixed, forever changing,
Laughing, weeping, douting, changing;
Wild, capricious, giddy, vain
Cloy'd with pleasure, nursed with pain;
Age steals on with wintry force
Ev'ry rapt'ous hope to chase,
Like a withered sapless tree,
Bowed to chilling fates decree;
Stripped of all its foliage gay,
Drooping at the close of day;
What of tedious life remains?
Keen regrets and careless pains;
Till death appears, a welcome friend,
To bid the scene of sorrow end."

S........B........ Athens, March 28th, 1831

(Samuel died in 1863 after spending forty-eight years in Athens during which time he was engaged in wool-carding and various

mills including oil, grist and sawmills. He was also a salt manufacturer. In addition, he served as an associate judge for one term.)

♦ ♦ ♦ ♦

Elvira P. Crippen: I am the daughter of Amos and Amelia (Steadman) Crippen, yet another of Athens' earliest families. I considered Harriet one of my very best friends. I still remember skipping rope and playing hide and seek in the groves as children. Harriet was an explorer even then. She was always dragging me off to the hills to play "Discover." I suppose I didn't find her decision to go west too surprising, what with that background.

When she confided to me that one day she would even see the Pacific Ocean and California, then a part of Mexico, I had no doubt she would at least try. However, when she said she would travel there overland, through miles and miles of hostile, unknown territory, well, that was sheer folly, I thought. Plenty of folks were heading to the territories back then but it was unthinkable for this well-to-do, young lady to even consider such a move. It was inviting disaster! Harriet's parents, from personal experience, knew the toils associated with settling new lands and wanted a more secure life for their daughter. Harriet was not raised to be a settler; she was expected to marry a gentleman and live in an eastern civilized town. Why she would choose to tempt fate in some godforsaken wilderness, when she need not do so, was beyond most of us.

Though I hoped for the best, I had a bad feeling. People disappeared in the West, leaving loved ones behind to fret. I was worried for my friend and wanted her to know she could count on me if ever in need.

To Harriet

Oft as thine eye shall fondly trace
The simple line I sketch for thee,
What ever the time what ever the place
Then think on me!
When pleasure sparkles in your eye,
And every scene is fair to see,
When swift the happy moments fly
Oh, think on me!
Thy life, thy bliss, may heaven defend,
But should'st thou by it's stern decree;
Ere want a true and faithful friend
Apply to me!

Elvira P. Crippen Athens April 8, 1831

(Elvira married Prince S. Baker September 8, 1836 in Athens. They had no children.)

♦ ♦ ♦ ♦

R.C. Pruden: Other than myself, Harriet was the favorite of father's seven daughters. My name is Rebecca, the fifth of twelve children, thirteen if you count Samuel. I was born May 6, 1808, in Washington County, Ohio.

Fate does indeed work in mysterious ways. For instance, Harriet's album might never have come to pass had my sister Aschah and I not visited relatives in Gambier, Ohio late in 1830. Gambier is in Knox County and is home to Kenyon College. Gambier these days is part of the Mt. Vernon metropolitan area. Mt. Vernon was the home of John Chapman, better known as Johnny Appleseed. He left Mt. Vernon in 1828 and relocated to Indiana to begin his horticultural adventure.

In any case, while we were visiting there, friends began a commonplace book for me. It was a popular pastime amongst the college students. Once we returned to Athens and mother saw my album and how much I treasured it she decided we should start an album for sister Harriet. My album was the inspiration for Harriet's.

One hundred and seventy-five years later my album is still with the family and is much loved. It now resides with my great-great nephew in Michigan, and, like Harriet's, my album also went on quite an adventure.

The poem I wrote to my sister brings back bittersweet memories. Harriet and I were very close. We enjoyed reading poetry together and she often confided in me. I disagreed with Harriet that the unknown West would be a grand adventure. I remembered our elders' stories of the toil and dangers they experienced when they were living as settlers. It was, to me, not an appealing lifestyle and I was worried for my sister's well-being. Emanuel wanted to take Harriet to Northern Indiana, a dangerous place in the early 1830's. That area was still flush with Indians. Emanuel was singing the syren's song, putting dangerous ideas in Harriet's head and leading her down a perfidious path, so he was barely tolerated by the family.

I knew that only "he who reigns above" could guard her in her chosen direction or welcome her in the next world. Reading my poem again after all these years I recall how fetching and sweet Harriet was. I hope I conveyed that.

Selected for Sister Harriet

O, thou who in thy early spring
Art bright, and sweet, and gay -
Who, blithe as birds, dost lightly sing
As free from care as they;

Around whose brow fair hope hath bound
A wreath of charmed flowers,
And led thee, like a victim crown'd,
To her deceitful bowers:

List, list not, to the syren's voice
Her words are light as air,
Today, with her thou may'st rejoice -
The next, weep with despair.

But place on him who reigns above,
The hope of thy young heart,
And thou shall triump in his love,
When earthly hopes depart.
Then faith shall be thy earthly guide
To his own holy heaven
And love shall ope the portals wide,
And joys untold be given

R.C. Pruden Prudensville, April 9th, 1831

(Please see the Postscript for more on Rebecca and her book.)

♦ ♦ ♦ ♦

A.C. Larak: I admit it, I was smitten with Miss Harriet Pruden. I had hoped to win her heart. Her mother, Mrs. Pruden, had an agreement with most of the professors at the University that they would help introduce her daughters to young men whom they considered to be with promise. Her mother was trying to distract Harriet from her interest in another young man, considered unworthy by the family. A.G. Brown insisted I accompany him to dinner at the Pruden residence one day after classes. I had no idea they were playing match-makers. All of the Pruden daughters were lovely, but Harriet stood out in my eyes. And it wasn't just the long flowing curls the color of honey, the wide brown eyes or her perfectly turned figure. No, there was something even more beautiful about Miss Pruden. She was engaging. She made whomever she was giving her attention to feel special. She always saw the best in people and was beyond kind or benevolent; she was angelic.

Harriet was also intelligent. She could hold her own in any discussion of politics or current events.

Miss Pruden enjoyed my company and I was invited back for dinner parties and the like. She and I on occasion took walks or carriage rides around their land. It was then I would try to woo her. I believe she found me amusing but harmless. Nonetheless, I did manage to steal a kiss, once. Unfortunately that was as far as my charm would take me. We remained friends but I never again tasted those sweet lips.

I suppose I was resentful and jealous of this Emanuel character. I had much more to offer her: a good life in a nice house in a secure town. I just could not believe that she would prefer *him*. Her heart however was in the West. It got so I would sulk about in my own despair, which only amused Harriet. She said that I would always be her dear friend but no more. I blurted out that I would no longer be available for visits. That blunder is why I called myself "folly's notary." Life became much less gay and I found myself regretting my rash decision. I felt sorry for myself. When I heard of Harriet's announcement I joined the group which had formed to create her 'shrine,' the poetry commonplace album.

Solitude

I love at evenings silent tide
When buzy care hath flown
In some sequestered dell to hide
And pensive muse alone.
Tis there in solitude refined
Reflection feels its part
Tis then the contemplative mind
With reasons charm is blest
Tis then the expanding soul ascends
And roves through fields above
Tis then the mystic essence blends
With unrepented love.
O Solitude, thy soothing charm
Can conquer fell despair
Can sad afflictions sting disarm

And banish every care
While folly's notary pens thy shrine
And grandeur fills thy breast
Still be thy rich enjoyments mine
To bless lifes fleeting hour

Larak AC   Athens April 19th 1831

♦ ♦ ♦ ♦

Louisa M. Fuller: It is no coincidence that my poem appears just after Mr. Larak's. I entered mine a day after AC and in that location in the album to show my solidarity with him. Do not misunderstand me, I loved Harriet as much as anyone. I admired her spirit, but I was angry that she had toyed with AC's heart and then given him the mitten. Mainly I suppose that I was angry because I did not want Harriet to leave us. I felt AC Larak a much more realistic choice for Harriet. He was handsome, ambitious and his family was well-to-do. With AC she would have wanted for nothing. I could not picture Harriet as a settler, no one could. She loved parties, socializing and fine clothes. Could she really give all that up to live in the wilderness where she would be making her own clothes!?

Friendship

A brighter rose never graced its tree
Than that which blossoms here for me;
Ne'er lingered joys delighted eye
Upon a milder evening sky,
Nor ever seemed beauty more serene
Than dwells on this enchanting scene.

Yet fairer than the fairest rose,
Than every flower that summer shows,
And milder than the pensive light
That lingers on the brow of night;

Than all earths dearer scenes more dear
Exists a charm I find not here.

Oh! Sweeter far is Friendship's sigh
Than thy breath of purity!
Thy dew drops shining mid the ray
That hails the summers fervid day;
Than these there dwells a charm more bright
In feelings eye of weeping light.

Then wonder not the wing of thought
That brighter dearer charm has sought,
Though oft I gaze delighted gaze,
On all the stores that earth displays,
There lives no one so sweet and dear,
As Friendship's smile as Friendship's tear.

Louisa M. Fuller Athens, April 20th, 1831

♦ ♦ ♦ ♦

Anonymous: My subject was friendship, as you can see. I counted myself among those who wanted to remember and be remembered by Miss Harriet. Her then upcoming adventure was most exciting and controversial. Harriet and her beau certainly livened things up in our otherwise tranquil little village.

If I ever catch the scoundrel who tore out the second half of my poem to Harriet, I'll give him a sound thrashing. I worked very hard on it, and don't mind saying it was well written.

Friendship

The smiling joys that around us play,
The airy hopes that rise
And throw around their vivid rays,

To check our murmuring sighs -
Combine within a social brest,
Which friendship's glowing light has blest.
Who would be doom'd to live alone,
Exploring contemplations field,
None but the wretch that's doomed to moan,
And seek in solitudes shield,
(Bottom half of page and poem are gone)

♦ ♦ ♦ ♦

Anonymous: What Harriet was doing was not just scandalous it was embarrassing for the whole village. She was carrying on with this unacceptable man and was actually considering going with him to live amongst the Indians and wild beasts! Some of us thought she had lost her mind. Up until that point Harriet had been the picture of perfection in a daughter. Her mother Mary, my good friend, was beside herself. If you ask me, that girl just needed a sound whipping, but that was not the Pruden way, hence Harriet's behavior was proceeding unchecked.

I thought the idea of the keepsake album would accomplish nothing as far as changing the girl's mind. I suppose it was worth a try though, and the class itself was quite enjoyable. Professor Brown was an excellent teacher and taught us all much about the rich tradition of commonplace books.

I composed this poem as an instructive statement for Harriet. I wanted to show her (despite her behavior) she had many friends who were trying to help her find a way out of her predicament. From my point of view, Harriet was letting down her friends and family. She was deserting the very people who had cared for her these many years. She was also carrying on in ways a proper young lady shouldn't. I did not sign the piece as I knew Harriet understood I did not approve, I wanted mine to be just an anonymous one of the many. The idea was to show her how many friends she had in Athens who did not want to see her leave. The point was not to chastise her, as I would have preferred.

Friendship

"Dwells there on earth a charm so sweet
As that which binds the human soul,
When we a kindred spirit greet
In confidence beyond control
Oh, no, its soft consoling power,
Dispels the lingering cloud of woe
Soothes us in many a pensive hour,
And bids our happiest feelings flow.
If sorrow wrings the heart with grief,
Or storms despair arise,
Fair friendship flies to give relief,
A ministering angel from the skies?"

♦ ♦ ♦ ♦

Lucy Knowles: One of the many things Harriet and I had in common was a love of poetry and a total inability to write our own. As I am sure you can tell, most of our friends could rhyme well, so it was somewhat embarrassing. Harriet and I didn't mind, we usually just giggled at our ineptness.

It was beyond belief that she was really going to do this thing, going to live in the wilderness. It scared me to death. I couldn't bear to part with my dear friend; perhaps never to see her again, which is exactly what happened. None of us, to my knowledge, ever saw her again after they left Ohio and ran off to the vastness of the West.

I agreed with Mrs. Pruden that a heartfelt intervention might convince Harriet to change her mind and stay in Athens. In the end Harriet would not be deterred, she would see and explore the West, one way or another. All she needed was a male partner, as women were not allowed to venture off by themselves in those days. She found that partner in Emanuel Light.

I searched and searched for just the right poem to give to Harriet for her album. I settled on one of Mr. Thomas Cambell's latest pieces. I know Harriet felt the same as I. We would miss each other terribly.

By the way, back in the 1800's, 'Lethe' was an oft-used word. Lethe is a mythical river in Hades whose water caused forgetfulness of the past for those who drank of it.

Absence

Tis not the loss of love's assurance
It is not doubting what thou art
But tis the too, too long endurance
Of absence that afflicts my heart

The fondest thoughts two hearts can cherish
When each is lonely doomed to weep
Are fruits on desert isles that perish
Or riches buried in the deep

What though, untouched by jealous madness
Our bosom's peace may fail to wreck
The undoubting heart that breaks with sadness
Is but more slowly doomed to break

Absence! Is not the soul torn by it
From more than light, or life or breath.
Tis Lethe's gloom, but not its quiet -
The pain without the peace of death

Athens April 21st 1831 Lucy Knowles

(Lucy Curtis Knowles was born March 10, 1818 at Little Hocking, Washington, Ohio and died January 15, 1899 in Alabama. She married John Wilston.)

♦ ♦ ♦ ♦

J.D.: I chose an entry with a time-honored truth both to and about Harriet. She was a most benevolent dear-heart and so my choice of a portion of Mr. James Beattie's essay seemed appropriate. Mr. Beattie lived in the 18th century. He was a poet, philosopher, man of letters and a favorite read in my own family.

Harriet seemed intent, in 1831, on leaving us soon. I hoped the album would accompany her and bring her comfort in the far away savage lands.

Benevolence

True benevolence is not a meteor which occasionally glare, but a luminary, which in its regular course diffuses all around its benign art influence.

The heart that feels for others woes,
Shall feel each selfless sorrow less;
Her heart who happiness bestows
Reflected happiness shall bless.

Would you experience the most exalted and rapturous sensations of which your nature is capable, give full scope to the impulses of benevolence; try what it is to heal the broken heart and to diffuse joy and gladness through the mansions of sorrow. Let thy flock cloth the naked, and thy table feed the hungry,

And from the prayer of want and plaint of woe,
O never never turn away thine ease;
Forlorn, in this bleak wilderness below,
Oh! What were man, should heav'n refuse to hear?

J.D.

♦ ♦ ♦ ♦

O.J. Honre: But of course I remember Harriet Pruden, she was *mon petite fleur.* In every way she was a flower. Her presence lingered like a flower's sweet perfume. A bright flower on a bed of grass will attract and hold the eye. So, too, did Harriet Pruden whenever she entered a room.

I was invited to the Pruden's for social functions, courtesy of my professors at the University. There I spent many happy hours. An entire small town had grown up around and associated with the Pruden's mills; Prudensville they used to call it. Most anyone who was anyone socialized at the Pruden household at one time or another so I was no one special in that regard. I did however get the distinct impression that I was being 'looked over' as it were, as a possible match for one of the daughters. I was immediately attracted to both Harriet and her older sister Aschah. Aschah had a regular beau, Mr. John Brough. He was then a typesetter but would eventually become the Governor of Ohio. Harriet was the one for whom I was being scrutinized and I was flattered. She was a delight, but alas, utterly uninterested *en moi.* I became yet another of the army of the rejected but nonetheless smitten with Miss Harriet Pruden. We suitors were hopeless and practically fell over each other to catch her eye, though we all knew it was to no avail. Her infatuation with that man infuriates me to this day! She was far too refined to be a settler and could not possibly survive out there for long. She had no experience with hard living. Sadly, Miss Pruden's wild dream became the flower of my poem.

The Fading Flower

It began to droop when the mid day's beam
On it's leafy beauties played
But I heeded it not for again twould seem
As lovely I thought, when the bright sun's gleam
Would sink in the twlight shade
And I waited to see how the cooling eve
Would its balmy sweets restore
But alas! Tho I saw the night breeze heave
Its breast, and the dew in its fair cup leave

Still it only drooped the more.
I marked it yet thro the darkening gloom
As it withered and lingered on
And twas lovely still, tho twould never resume
Its former pride -tho its budding bloom
And its balmy seetes were gone.
At length, as it faded and pined away
The pale moon glimmered round
And it beamed where the sinking flowerlet lay
And I saw its leaves by the pale moon ray
Strewed senseless on the ground
And alas! (as I stooped where low twas laid)
Is it thus I thought will flee
The vision of bliss, by hope's gay beam made,
Is it thus the wild dreams of the young heart fade
And bloom but a day like thee?

O.J. Honre Athens, April 25th Anno Domino 1831

♦ ♦ ♦ ♦

B.S. Shipman: I am the son of Colonel Charles Shipman, who settled in Athens in 1813. He prospered in merchandising and gave me a good upbringing. Harriet and I were virtually the same age. What you have to understand about Harriet's choice to head to the territories is just how rare it was for a refined young lady to even consider such an endeavor. Yes, many people were going west. They were, by and large, people who did not own land in the East, which was getting scarce. The less fortunate's only chance to own land was in the West. Harriet's people owned land and continued to prosper in Ohio. She had no need to leave us, save for adventure. She was just ahead of her time, and lest we forget, she was in love.

Though many a joy around thee smile,
And many a faithful friend you meet,
Where love may cheer life's dreary way,
And turn the bitter cup to sweet?

Let memory sometimes bear thee back
To other days almost forgot,
And when thou think'st of other friends
Who love thee well - forget me not!

B.S. Shipman, Athens, April 28, 1831

♦ ♦ ♦ ♦

N.L.B.: I was one of the few people in Athens who believed in Harriet's choices, both in a lifestyle and choice for a husband. Most in Athens felt Harriet was being led naively down a road to unknown misery, though some, myself included, admired her moxie. It was my belief that Destiny had truly brought those two together for the purpose of exploring the West and there making their mark. It really was quite the storybook romance...penniless boy and affluent girl, with a common dream, they meet by chance and inevitably fall in love despite all those who worked hard to derail their plans. I knew it could work out tragically for Harriet. Nonetheless, she could perish in a civilized town just as easily from childbirth, or a million and one other causes, as she could in the wilderness.

In my poem, Harriet and Emanuel are the "wild kindred nature's" who were indeed "too long detained apart." I was referring to the six long years for them in Athens, when they tried to make a go of it. They would never have been truly accepted in Athens, leaving the wilderness and the young couple's hope for love and happiness, inextricably bound.

As the waves from distant fountains
Rolling onwards to the main,
After wandering 'mid the mountains
Mingle sweetly o'er the plain -

Even so wild kindred natures -
Tho too long detained apart;
And unknowing form and features -
When they must, unite in heart N.L.B.

♦ ♦ ♦ ♦

Niore C.B.: Harriet and I were having a picnic beside the Hocking river when I wrote her my remembrance poem. It was a perfect day, clear and bright. The birds were singing and we sat nibbling on sweets, reading poetry and dipping our toes in the river. I wanted Harriet to remember this moment of peace and happiness from her hometown. Incidentally, the reference to "foney's finger" was a play on the word Fons who was the ancient Roman god of springs. I was saying our river was Foney's finger.

Before thee let one vision linger
Made brighter still by foney's finger
A scene like this, oh, may it be -
Then - oh, then remember me.

Athens, May 1834   Niore C.B.....

♦ ♦ ♦ ♦

O.C.C.: My sister and I played with Harriet and her siblings when we were all young so she was like another sister to us. Harriet and I wept together when she told me of her plans. We both knew it would be hard to be separated. She was so ambitious and wanted to be one of the first to see the unexplored country. Nothing we could do would change her mind. Most of us did not have Harriet's gumption. She was virtually the only female of the older, wealthier Athens families who, in those early days, wanted to venture even farther west. I admired her greatly. She stuck to her guns despite the considerable pressure working to thwart her plans.

Smile on thou wert not form'd for tears;
And if their trace hath been
Upon thy cheek; in those bright years
When life's first hopes were green;

They were as the fostering dew
Upon the young flowers bloom;
Which nourisheth its grace of hue
And richness of perfume.
Smile on! For blest shall be thy lot,
And brilliant thy career,
Oh! Sure the world can offer not
A fairer promise here;;

O.C.C.

♦ ♦ ♦ ♦

Olivia: I am pleased to see how faded my poem to Harriet is. It indicates it was out in the sun often, being read. I had hoped my contribution would please Harriet. It is a poem about what I saw as the three phases of life: youth, adulthood and old age. Harriet was my model for the middle phase. She had to steal away to the woods to be with her true love, and as the poem suggests, she did not at first confide with her friends about her illicit love affair. Eventually it became public knowledge, but for the first few months the couple attempted to keep their love a secret. They knew it would unleash a storm of protest and gossip. However, they were not fooling anyone. Athens was still just a small village and as such it was almost impossible to keep a secret. Her "varying cheek" did indeed tell the tale.

The Three Homes

"Where is thy home?" I asked a child,
Who, in the morning air
Was twining flowers most sweet and wild
In garlands for her hair.
"My home" the happy heart replied
And smiled in childish glee,
"Is on the sunny mountain side
Where soft winds wander free."

O blessings fall on artless youth,
And all its rosy hours,
When every world is joy & truth,
And treasures live in flowers!

"Where is thy home" I asked of one
Who bent, with flushing face
To hear a warriors tender tone
In the wild woods secret place.

She spoke not, but her varying cheek
The tale might well impart
The home of her young spirit meek
Was in a kindred heart.

Ah! Souls that well might soar above
To earth will fondly cling
And build their hopes on human love,
That light and fragile thing!

"Where is thy home, thou lonely man?"
I asked a pilgrim gray,
Who came with furrowed brow, & was
Slow musing on his way.
He paused and with a solemn voice
Upturned his holy eyes
"The land I seek thou never hast seen,
My home is in the skies!"

O! Blest -thrice blest! Her heart must be
When such thoughts are given,
That walks from worldly fetters free
His only home in heaven!

June 10th 1831 Olivia

♦ ♦ ♦ ♦

M.E.H.: My poem may not be the best in Harriet's album, I do think, however, it accurately reflects the thinking of many people of that time. As one of the others mentioned, "change is and is to be." We all knew that in the 1800's, we just did not like it. Life was too tenuous in those days. Change of any kind more often than not meant something bad in the making. People wanted security not change, constancy not uncertainty. That is why we envisioned Heaven as a place where change did not occur. In Heaven friends did not leave, never to be seen again, as was the case with Harriet and Emanuel. Once they left Logan they were gone from our lives for good. All we had was our faith that we would be reunited with our dear friends when "earthly scenes are flown."

The Eye of Faith

For in the eye of faith may view
A type of, that righter and kinder day
When the winter of life pass'd away
And the saints shall all join in the song
That the winter of life is past away
And we all are with jesus at home
And when life's summer sun is past
And earthly scenes are flown
O! May I reign with thee at last
Where changes are not known

M.E.H.

♦ ♦ ♦ ♦

B.L. Miles: My sister Lucy and I were pleased to participate in the making of Harriet's album. We were all moved to write poems for Harriet. First, because she always inspired us with her beauty and fine character and second because she was willing to give up her comfortable life to venture into the unknown. Everyone knew we might never hear from her again.

We perceived her ambition as a combination of bravery and courage, powered (and blinded) by love. Many, myself included, felt compelled to show our affection for Harriet. We wanted to say goodbye and to thank her for the delight she brought to us all during her years in Athens.

While wandering down the wandering stream of time
The days and years successive roll;
May friendship's sun upon thee shine,
And cheer thy soul

May fortune's star propitious gleam
With brillant lustre o'er thy head;
And o'er thy mind wisdom beam
Its radiance shed.

May every season bring thee health,
And joys the purest most refined;
May heaven bestow the richest wealth
A tranquil mind

Transcribed by your friend
Athens, July 11 1831 B.L. Miles

♦ ♦ ♦ ♦

Lucy t.d. Miles: As my brother B.L. said, we were happy to be a part of the group that began Harriet's album. Who would have guessed the little book would last so long and visit so many places?

My people lived in Athens. My father and his brother, JB (Joseph) and RW Miles, bought Prudensville from the Prudens in 1836, the year Harriet left Athens. Harriet was a sensation to everyone in her hometown. She was a dazzling natural beauty but not overly vain. She was smart and engaging with a quick wit. I admired her, and wanted her to know it, however I wanted to say it subtly in my poem. When I wrote, "Thy virtuous wish, the purpose high..." I meant it as a message to Harriet. I hoped Mrs. Pruden would not catch on. She did not approve of her daughter's dream or choice of a man.

But honestly, I did not give Harriet much of a chance of surviving in the wild woods. She was too petite and not built for or used to toil; I didn't know what her fate would be. I only knew that Harriet's beauty would fade but her memory would live on with her friends, if indeed she was to leave on her 'adventure,' as she called it; which of course, she did.

Sweet flower, so young, so fresh, so fair,
Bright pleasure sparkling in thine eye,
Alas! Even thee time will not spare
And thou must die.
That heart with youthful hopes so gay
That scarcely ever breathed a sigh
Must weep o'er pleasures fled away;
For all must die
But though the roseate cheek may fade,
Thy virtuous wish, the purpose high,
The bloom with which the soul's arrayed
Shall never die.

Lucy t.d. Miles

♦ ♦ ♦ ♦

Silas M Pruden: I was born in Morristown, New Jersey, in 1773. My second wife Mary (Bingham) was born in Athens. We met in Washington County, Pennsylvania and were married there June 25, 1801. Our move to Athens in 1814 was a year before Harriet was born. I purchased the mills and farm of Jehiel Gregory east of Athens, improved them and there made a good living. Mary and I were happy in Athens and raised six sons and seven daughters.

My wife was dead set against Harriet marrying this Light fellow. First, she was so very young, only sixteen in 1831.

Second, Emanuel was threatening to drag her off into the lawless wilderness. Third, my wife felt Emanuel unworthy of our favorite daughter. I for one liked Mr. Light and tried to persuade him to work for me and stay in Ohio. He was a hard worker and an honest young man though lacking any formal education. I felt they would eventually be accepted, as long as Harriet did not become a fallen woman.

It was not to be, however, and in the summer of 1836 they eloped and moved to Logan, up in Hocking County. Mary and I also moved to Logan in 1837, in part due to my wife's mortification over the scandal the elopement brought but also due to the financial crash of that year. We were almost bankrupt. We sold everything we could and departed Athens, leaving many friends. My son Samuel remained and prospered. I was not part of the group which gathered in 1831 to create Harriet's Remembrance Album but did enter my own poem later in the summer of that same year. My message to Harriet was to be careful in planning for her future. Even if it seems rosy, a bright future can have a way of becoming something one does not desire.

"I cannot stain this snowy leaf
Without a sigh of pensive grief
As musing on my days gone by,
and those that still before me lie
I read a mournful emblem here,
That few could read without a tear.
For as my musing eyes I cast
Upon the pages that are past
I search them all, but search in vain
To find just one without a stain!
But what has been is not to be –
The happy future yet is free,
Far as my forward eye can go,
The future still is white as snow
So free from stains so free from cares,
The tainted past it half repairs
It is a goodly sight! But oh!
Too well within the heart I know

That this fair future; at the last,
Shall be itself the tainted past"
S...M...P... Prudensville Aug. 9th, 1831

(Silas died on November 30, 1856, he was then 83 years old. He was associated closely with the Presbyterian church, both in Athens and in Logan.)

♦ ♦ ♦ ♦

Mary Hildreth: Friendship was one of the most important things in life back in those days. Not that it is not important now, it is just that friendship then was often one's only support. We had very little of what people take for granted today. Without true friends one was in trouble when hard times arose, which was more often than not.

Harriet was very comely and adored by all. I tell you, it is no exaggeration. As you can see from my poem I considered her a true friend. I felt a strong bond with her, we were kindred spirits and I missed her deeply when she departed.

My father, Dr. Samuel P. Hildreth, attended Ohio University between 1822 and 1825. The Prudens were closely associated with OU, and we became acquainted with their family soon after arriving in Athens. My family returned to Marietta, Ohio after my father graduated. It is about forty miles away from Athens. He returned frequently on business and I accompanied him as often as I could for the opportunity just to visit with my Harriet.

To Miss H........P............

Friendship how cheering is that sound
To those who know its meaning true;
And yet how few on earth are found,
Who've felt its charms - alas! Too few
Yet thousands shout the magic word
And boast the sacred name of Friend

But let misfortune's croak be heard,
And soon their friendships at an end.
With such tis mockery - a show
A dream - a simple tag
Yet such as these can never know
The bliss that friends enjoy.
Those only, who with hearts the same,
At Friendship's holy altar kneel -
Know the true meaning of that name;
The sainted joy all true friends feel

Inserted by your friend
M.H.
Athens, Oct 16th 1831

♦ ♦ ♦ ♦

Mary Hildreth: This was my final poem to Harriet, written in 1834, as I recollect. My two other poems were longer (above and page 74). I wanted to add a short piece, one that would be lyrical, fun and easy to remember but heartfelt, so she would know how much I wished her well and would miss her.

When you have sought some favorite spot
A summers eve in mirth to spend,
Will you then cast a lingering thought
On one who's now an absent friend
M.H.

(Mary Ann Hildreth was born around 1808 in Marietta, Washington County, Ohio. She married Douglas Putnam February 16, 1831. She died at an early age on October 24, 1842 in Marietta.)

♦ ♦ ♦ ♦

Aschah Pruden: I wrote this poem thinking of my sister Harriet. She never realized what a rare beauty she was. She understood she was pretty and had many boys tripping over each other to prove it. She enjoyed nice clothes and other frilly things as much as other girls, but she wasn't obsessed with them like many her age. Mother saw to it that Harriet was groomed to marry well, like the rest of us girls. We were all (I don't mind saying) perfect social graces. Our mother wanted us to have what she had not when she was our age. Harriet always did what was expected of her but it wasn't really important to her; she would rather have her nose in a book or magazine. All of us girls were indoctrinated into the Cult of Domesticity of True Womanhood so even Harriet's constant reading was worrisome. It was believed that education took away twenty percent of a woman's 'vital forces' and thus could harm her reproductive abilities.

My sister was a rose who did not understand what an effect she had on virtually everyone she ever met. She saw herself as no different from the other girls, just another rose. I wonder if she ever understood she was an exceptional flower.

ATHENS Feb 8th 1836

The Rose

I am the one rich thing that morn
Leaves for the ardent noon to win;
Grasp me not, I have a thorn.
But bend and take my fragrance in.

The dew drops on my bosom gives
The whole of Heaven to searching eyes;
Only he who sees it lives
And only he who slights it dies.

Petal on petal opening wide
My being into beauty flows

Hundred - leaved and damask - dyed -
Yet nothing, nothing but a rose!

♦ ♦ ♦ ♦

Louise: Harriet threw caution to the wind both in her lifestyle choice and love life; she made up her own mind in all things. We girls were expected to grow up to be the wives and mothers that our parents wanted us to be. We were to marry well and live for and be supportive of our husbands' ambitions, not our own. Thus Harriet had to swim upriver against a powerful current to achieve her ambitions. She chose to go against almost everything that was the norm at the time. It caused a scandal which she rode out.

I did not write this poem and cannot remember for the life of me who did.

When summer decks thy path with flowers
And pleasure's smile is sweetest
When not a cloud above thee bows
And sunshine leads thy happy hours
Thy happiest and thy fleetest
O! Watch thou lest pleasures smile
Thy spirit of its hope beguile

When roused the gathering storms are nigh
And grief thy days has shaded
When earthly joys bloom but to die
And tears suffuse thy eye
And hopes bright bow hath faded
Oh! Walk thou then lest anxious care
Invade thy breast and rankle there

Through all life's scenes, through zeal and woe
Through days of mirth and gladness;
Where (*oft*) thy wandering footsteps go oh!

Think how transient here below
Thy sorrow and thy sadness
And watch them always! Lest thou stray
From him who points thy heavenward way

Louise

(This poem was published in a Wisconsin newspaper, in 1957, under the title, "Watch Ye!")

♦ ♦ ♦ ♦

Aschah Pruden: This little love poem was given me, inscribed on a card, by my then future husband, Mr. John Brough. He was a mere typesetter in 1831, but I knew he had great things in store in his future. Harriet's album was begun because of love, even if misplaced. For that reason I thought it appropriate to enter this sweet saying. Harriet was my younger sister, we were also confidantes. She was so happy for me when Mr. Brough began seriously courting me.

Sweet was the day, and sweet the hour
When cupid made me own thy power.

♦ ♦ ♦ ♦

Maxon: Actually it is Ann Maxon but most just called me by my last name. My family immigrated to this country in 1801, from Scotland, almost thirty years before I wrote this poem. By 1831, I was thirty-five and was the sole remaining member of my clan. I was married for a brief time but my man died and I had no children of my own. I always felt Harriet was my 'adopted' child but we were also the best of friends and spent many happy hours together. I worked for her parents, cleaning and cooking. They always treated me well, paid me an honest wage and provided me with room and board in the form of a small cabin in Prudensville.

Once Emanuel Light arrived on the scene, things got interesting in Athens. Miss Harriet was not raised to marry a poor man and run off to the wild woods. Oh no, that was not the idea at all, not the plan. Have you noticed that plans we have for others seldom work out as we envision them? As for myself, I thought Mr. Light a grand lad with much promise in spite of his lack of pedigree (which mattered not a whit to Harriet or me). Of course, I could never say that out loud without suffering the wrath of Mrs. Pruden, so I kept my mouth shut around her.

At first they had their own 'Underground Railroad,' with me as the train. I passed messages back and forth. I delivered letters to Harriet (with great discretion) that Emanuel wrote from out of town. Generally I acted as their go-between. I was lucky my neck was not wrung! When Harriet finally went public with the news it was a great relief to me.

Most people looked at Harriet as naive and innocent but they did not really know her. She had made up her mind, shortly after she learned to read, that adventure and exploration would be her life's work. Quite an ambition when women seldom had a say about anything. Harriet's bravado, her sense of independence was well ahead of her time. In 1831 it caused a sensation. It had simply not occurred to anyone that a young lady like Harriet would *want* to marry 'down' or that she would *prefer* to live a hard life when she could have lived a life of relative luxury and security.

Emanuel was everything Harriet had ever wanted. He was a big, strong, strapping lad with a sharp mind and wit. More importantly, he had no attachments to keep him from venturing west. He was not wealthy and did not own land in the East. Additionally, he had relatives who at the time were starting out for the wilds of Northern Indiana or were already there. All he needed was a small push to be convinced to join them. Harriet gave him a shove.

Emanuel, like Harriet, had read everything he could about the West. They talked for hours on end about what it would be like 'out there', and what there was to see and experience.

What with all the goings-on regarding *Amor*, I thought a wee poem to Harriet about how to choose the right man was appropriate. So I composed this one for the dear.

To Miss Harriet Pruden
(ay, and other young ladies)

Detest disguise; remember tis your part
By gentle fondness to retain the heart,
Let duty, prudence, virtue take the lead
To fix your choice – but from it never recede.
Despise coquetry – spurn the shallow fool
Who measures out dull compliments by rule,
And without meaning, like a chattering jay,
Repeats the same dull strains throughout the day.
Are men of sense attracted by your face,
Your well turned figure, or this compound grace?..
"Be mild and equal, moderately gay,
Your judgement rather than your wit display"

Inscribed by your friend Maxon

Athens Oct. 22, 1831

♦ ♦ ♦ ♦

Maxon: This poem to Miss Harriet is the only one I did not write myself, it is by Reginald Heber (1783-1826). The correct title is *On Heavenly and Earthly Hope.* I hoped for the best for my friend, but earthly hope is uncertain and restless. I found comfort knowing that one as pure as she would find heavenly hope certain when her time came. I did not know what the future had in store for my young friend, all I knew was she was taking a terrible risk as she ventured into the land of uncertainty.

Hope

"Reflected on the lake I love
To see the stars of heaven glow,
Lo tranquil in the heaven above,
Lo restless in the wave below.

This heavenly hope is all serene,
But earthly hope is ever there;
Still flutters o'er this changing scene,
As false as fleeting as 'tis fair."

Athens, 22nd, Oct. 1831 Maxon

♦ ♦ ♦ ♦

R.A. Maxon: I wrote five poems to Harriet back in 1831, which should give you an indication of how much that dear-heart meant to me. I feared that I would become a distant memory for Harriet or be forgotten altogether. She was young and spirited and heading off on the adventure of her life. She would make many new friends along the way, why should she remember an old woman like me? I hoped I would remain a small part of her recollections as her days went by.

Ironically, as it turned out, my prediction (in the last four lines) came true, these few poems in this little album are the *only* historical record of my existence.

Within this hallowed shrine;
To think that oer these times thine eye
May wander in some future year,
And memory breathe a passing sigh
For her who traced them here.
Calm sleeps the sea when storms are over,
With bosom silent and serene,
And but the plank upon the shore
Reveals that wrecks have been.

So some frail leaf like this may be
Left floating on time's silent tide,
The sole remaining trace of me,
To tell I lived and died.

Athens Oct 28th, 1831 R.A. Maxon

♦ ♦ ♦ ♦

Ann Maxon: This is my least favorite poem, upon review. It is heartfelt, but without literary distinction, which I always strived for in my verse. I might have to rewrite it, in my next life. Of course it was written when I was feeling sorry for myself. Harriet was undeniably leaving Athens, and me, and I was sorrowful. My life would be lonely without Harriet, she was my best friend. She had so many, but I had only her as a true friend.

On Solitude

Oh! For some lonely dwelling place
Far from the haunts of men;
Where I might pass life's fleeting days;
Forgotten and unseen.

A cell or cave by nature form'd,
On some rude mountain's brow,
Blest with one friend, no more I'd ask,
While wandering here below.

With that dear friend, how sweet to stray
Along the winding stream,
As it is hastening to the main,
Beneath mild Cynthia's beam

Or in some shady grove reclin'd,
Far, far from noise and strife,

Like the sweet stream to glide in peace,
Down to the verge of life.

No prowling beast, no cruel bird,
No reptile should be there,
But innocence, and joy, and love
Reign undisturbed by care.

Ann Maxon

♦ ♦ ♦ ♦

R.A. Maxon: I hope you can tell from this poem just how much I would miss this young woman. As I reread my words a picture of Harriet appears in my mind, she was so fresh and young, perfectly formed and (I quote myself) "pure, ardent and kind." Though I would not see her again, in this life, I never did forget her. I knew not what fate would befall Harriet but always dreamed she made it, all the way to the West, to the Pacific Ocean, just like her heroes, Mr. Lewis and Mr. Clark. It brought me cheer to think she had.

To Miss Harriet

Though many a dull care may beset me
Before I behold thee again
Yet think not I ere can forget thee
Till reason has broken her chain.

No, never - a heart that has cherish'd
True love for a being like thee,
Will love on, till each feeling has perished
And memory ceases to be.

Thy throbbing and soft heaving bosom,
Thy flowing and negligent curl,
Thy cheek, with the rose's fresh blossom
First made me admire thee, sweet girl.

But though thee are angel like lovely,
And thy heart is pure ardent and kind,
Yet never did I know how to love thee,
Till I learned the sweet traits in my mind.

Then though many a dull care may beset me
Before I behold thee again,
Yet think not I ere can forget thee,
Till reason has broken her chain
R.A. Maxon

♦ ♦ ♦ ♦

Anonymous: In Athens we had all heard the stories, or knew from personal experience, of the hardships settlers found trying to clear and tame new lands. I just could not imagine sweet Harriet in that situation. Harriet's people and many of her friends' parents were themselves pioneer settlers, and proud of their past. Most, however, did not want their children, especially female children, to have to go through the same hardship. Harriet was determined to go and see for herself and that she did. Not having the town's favorite daughter around to brighten our days was a loss to us all. All I could do was write this little verse which I hoped would express to her the fear we all felt.

Parting

When forced to part from those we love,
Though sure to meet tomorrow,
We yet a kind of anguish prove
And feel a touch of sorrow,
But oh, what words can paint the fear
When from those friends we sever,

Perhaps to part for months for years -
Perhaps to part forever.

Athens Dec 15th 1831

♦ ♦ ♦ ♦

P.L. McAboy: Paradise Lynn McAboy, at your service. I graduated from Ohio University in 1835 and so was in Athens during a good bit of the Harriet Pruden affair. Silas and Mary Pruden asked me to try and intervene and derail Harriet's plans of going west. Many of us felt Harriet was overly infatuated with the West and Mr. Light. I, too, thought Harriet was making a huge mistake. The tendency of young adults to place too much faith in earthly pleasures was thought to be the driving force behind Harriet's dream. Silas and Mary felt that if we could just get her through that phase she would come to her senses and accept the path her parents had in mind for her. I chose this quote from Robert Burns to try and illustrate the point about the transient pleasures of youth: they don't last.

"Pleasures are like poppies spread,
You seize the flower, its bloom is shed,
Or like the snow-fall in the river,
A moment white then melts forever;
Or like the borealis race,
That flit ere you can point the place
Or like the rainbows lovely form
Vanishing amid the storm -
No man can tether time or tide" - Burns
Athens Sept 5th, 1833 P.L. McAboy

♦ ♦ ♦ ♦

P.L. McAboy: I felt it appropriate that the final leaf in Harriet's album should have an entry from Athens and the 1830's, so that no matter where she went she would eventually return to Ohio, at least in her book. I had no idea back then what a fantastic adventure the old album would have over its eighty years of active use.

I will always remember Harriet as a young dreamer, one who elected to take a path she chose for herself rather than the safe path others had chosen for her. My final apothegm is from the Old Testament, Ecclesiastes 12:1.

Stranger's Leaf -

"Remember now thy Creator in the days
Of thy youth"

P.L. McAboy

(PL would die in 1839 in Kentucky, the same year Harriet's first child was born. This quote, along with C.B.'s contribution [see p.66] are on the final sheet of the old album.)

♦ ♦ ♦ ♦

Jonathon Perkins Weethee: I was a relatively young man when I knew Harriet and her family. I remember them all well. After I graduated from Ohio University in 1832 I became a clergyman. Later I would become President of three different colleges: Madison College, Pennsylvania (1836), Beverly College, Ohio (1842), and Waynesburg College, Pennsylvania (1854). I would return to Athens throughout my life for business and pleasure.

My message to Harriet was that one should not put too much stock in earthly pleasures as they are temporary and unreliable over the long run. I understood the pleasures of being young and in love so I tried to be honest with Harriet when I told her, "they'll do awhile to sport upon/But not to love so fervently." I wanted Harriet to know that I understood her predicament. Passion is a strong force, especially the throes of young love. It was practically Shakespearean, a Romeo and Juliet drama unfolding in our little village. Two unlikely lovers nevertheless find each other. It was my hope Harriet would come to her senses and not venture off to the wilds of America. I tried to poetically convince her that these dreams of young love seldom work out. Like many of the other Athens 'poets' I reminded Harriet of the fleeting nature of life and pleasure. In the end, the only certainty, the only thing to cling to, is one's faith, not youthful fancy.

Cling not to Earth

Cling not to earth - theres nothing there,
However loved!! However fair,
But on its features still must wear
The impress of mortality
The voyager on boundless deep
Within his barque may smile or sleep -
But bear him on - he will not weep
To leave its wild uncertainty.
Cling not to earth - as soon we may
Trust Asia's serpents wanton play
That glitters only to betray
To death or else to misery.
Dream not of friendship - there may be
A word, a smile, a grasp for thee -
But wait the hour of need - and see -
But wonder not - their fallacy.
Think not of beauty - like the rest
It bears a lustre on its crest -
But short the time ere stands confest
Its falsehood - or its frailty.
Then rest no more so fondly on
The flowers of earth around thee strewn
They'll do awhile to sport upon
But not to love so fervently

Athens Sept 6th 1833 J.P. Weethee

♦ ♦ ♦ ♦

Jonathon Perkins Weethee: I penned three poems in Miss Pruden's commonplace book over a two day period. The first, which you have read, was written specifically for Harriet and the occasion. The following two short poems are from my own commonplace book. I always found them to be good guides for living my life, and hoped Harriet would appreciate them for the same reason. The first one truly was appropriate for Harriet, considering her above average looks. Peace of mind, harmony within, friendship and contentment, these things of substance should be valued more than fleeting pleasures. Incidentally, "chimie" is a play on the word chymic, a 16th century alchemist. You may also wonder about the reference to "Indian mines." India was where most large precious stones were mined in those days.

Beauty

What is the blooming tincture of a skin
To peace of mind, to harmony, within?
What the bright sparkling of the finest eye
To the soft soothing of a calm reply?
Can comliness of form, or shape, or (*h*)air
With comliness of words or deeds compare?
No. Those at first the unwary heart may obtain
But these, these only can that heart retain

Athens Sept 5th 1833 J.P. Weethee

There is a jewel which no indian mines can buy
No chimie art can counterfeit;
It makes men rich in greatest poverty,
Makes water wine, turns wooden cups to gold,
The homely whistle to sweet music's strain;

Seldom it comes, to few from Heaven sent,
That much in little - all in nought – content

Athens Sept 6th 1833 J.P.W.

♦ ♦ ♦ ♦

A.V. Medbery: While attending Ohio University I met the Pruden family. I attended between 1834 and 1839. This poem was written by William Cowper in 1782. It seemed appropriate for Miss Harriet's album as an apothegm. Commonplace books typically contained apothegms (also known as commonplaces,) for the owner to refer to.

"The lapse of time and rivers is the same,
Both spend their journey with a restless stream;
The silent pace with which they steal away,
No wealth can bribe, no pray'rs persuade to stay;
Alike irrevocable both when past,
And a wide ocean swallows both at last.
Though each resemble each in every part
A difference strikes at length the musing heart;
Streams never flow in vain; where streams abound,
Flow leaves the land with various plenty crown'd!
But time, that should enrich the nobler mind,
Neglected leaves a dreary waste behind."

A.V. Medbery
Athens Sept 21st 1833

♦ ♦ ♦ ♦

Lucy t.d. Miles: As I mentioned at my previous poem, I admired Harriet and her ambition. She truly inspired us all, even if we did not agree with her. When I wrote this I was fretting over Harriet. I was certain "youth's fond hope" would do her in. That is what I predicted in my poem. We young women who wrote poems to Harriet also had our own youthful hopes and dreams but they were modest compared to Harriet's. We did not want to go farther west until it was settled. Security is what we were taught to look for in life, love was almost secondary. You see, love was an earthly pleasure and as such was considered fleeting. Fleeting things are uncertain and therefore not secure. Harriet would not accept this idea. She felt love would shield her from the toils of life like a knight's armor and provide all the security she would need. It was as if she had blinders on which would not permit her to see she was choosing a road which could easily lead to her doom.

It had been almost three years since Harriet had announced her intentions and since the creation of her album. And still we could not convince her to stay with us and make a permanent life here in Athens. On the other hand she had not left us yet, which was a positive sign. To be sure, she had second thoughts. When Emanuel was not around we worked on her. We talked with her and tried to make her see the danger in her chosen course of action. Then he would return with new stories of the West...endless open spaces, sights never before seen, land rich with bounty. After a few days with Emanuel, all our good counsel was for naught.

Youth's Fond Hope

Nor smiles nor tears on childhood's cheek
A lasting joy or we bespeak
Joy then can nothing joys impart
The deepest feelings of the heart
A feather's weight may counter poise
Alike its little grief and joys

But when - our childhood years gone by
Kind nature offers her purpose high
The soul then wakes to nobler cause
A wider sphere of actions claim

New powers acquire - from day to day
And childhood's baubles cast away.

Then raises the immortal wind
With longings ardent undefined,
All forms on earth attract the eye
And into that gem the vaulted sky,
On natures and on fortunes course
Centers her intellectual force
Till fired imagination glows
And strong the tide of feeling flows
With every sense the heart can give
Of what it is, to be - to live

That matin dawn of life how fair!
How blithe how buoyant void of care!
Then youthful fancy fondly dreams
The world is ever as it seems
That pleasure's newly tasted bowl
Has power to satisfy the soul!
That good supreme dwells here below
And fortune can such boon bestow.

Alas! The lot by fate decreed
Such hope shall prove a broken reed
The power to enjoy but power to know
The anguish of a deeper - woe!
For not on earth exists the spot
Where disappointment enters not,
And he whose final hope is vain
Shall taste the poignancy of pain.
Thy guarantee of earthly joys
An earth soon trust - fond youth destroys

Lucy t.d.... Nov 1833

♦ ♦ ♦ ♦

A.A.L.: Many people, myself included, suspected that Miss Harriet would not long survive in the wilderness. We hoped we were wrong but nonetheless death was a very real possibility for a settler. Everyone knew it. Hence many people's thoughts turned to the afterlife and became the theme of many of the poems, mine included. We all worried about Harriet but knew, because of her benevolent nature, that she would find herself welcomed above when things became too hard for her here on earth.

Harriet and I had in common differing views of heaven from your average 19th century American. Many people then envisioned heaven as a place where one is physically the same but all earthly troubles are left behind (please see the poem by Lucy M. Nye which illustrates my point). Harriet, on the other hand, believed in heaven but also believed it possible to find heaven on earth. I believed heaven was a place where just the soul ascended and left the mortal, physical self behind.

The Mind

1st Yes - I shall change and fade away,
And though I change I shall not die
For mind shall triumph o'er decay,
Unquenched in light – eternity!
The grave may quench the body's breath,
But spirit cannot taste of death.

2nd The soul will dwell in mystic light
With not a thought to mar its bliss;
And in that world so purely bright
It will not even dream of this.
The grave may quench the body's breath,
But spirit cannot taste of death.

3rd Mind - vast expanse of life and light
Rolling within its earthly bed,
Reflects by turns the day - the night -
The joys we feel - the tears we shed.

The grave may quench the body's breath,
But spirit cannot taste of death.

4th How brief is life! Its utmost years -
Its breath commingling with distress!
It was - now is - now disappears -
A spirit in its nakedness.
The grave may quench the body's breath,
But spirit cannot taste of death.

5th The heavenly life is second birth;
By spirit - spirit is refined;
Flesh will resolve itself in earth,
And mind ascend to purer mind.
The grave may quench the body's breath,
But spirit cannot taste of death.

Inserted by your friend A.A.L.

Athens Nov 15 1833

♦ ♦ ♦ ♦

Mary A. Currier: Adaline was my sister, you read her poems earlier. I, too, was afraid for our friend Harriet; she had been bewitched and did not realize what she was doing. Of course she was quite young and was experiencing those 'new feelings.' In our Miss Pruden's case they seemed to be out of control and leading her into harm's way. Harriet's life in Athens had been "a sleepy lake." Life in the West would be a gale and soon her cheek would be "sorrowed by weeping," or so many of us thought.

Tide of Life

I saw while the earth was at rest,
And the curtains of heaven were glowing

A breeze full of balm from the West
O'er the face of a sleepy lake blowing.
It puffed a wave on its shore,
And the stillness to billows was broken;
The gale left it calm as before;
It slept as if never awoken.

Not thus with the dull tide of life;
One cheek may be sorrowed by weeping,
While free from the tempests of strife,
Another in peace may be sleeping
The wave once disturb'd by the breeze,
Can tranquilly sleep again never,
Till destiny chill it and freeze
The calm it had broken forever.

June 17, 1834 Mary A. Currier

♦ ♦ ♦ ♦

John Brough: I was Ohio's governor during a part of the War between the States and am still proud of my contribution to the Union effort. That was almost thirty years after I wrote this poem to my dear sister-in-law, Harriet Pruden. I married her sister, Aschah Pruden, in 1832. Sweet Aschah died tragically young at twenty-five years of age, in 1838.

In 1831 I was a typesetter working for A.G. Brown at his newspaper, *The Athens Mirror*. Mr. Brown introduced me to the Pruden family. As I hope you can tell from the tone and message of my poem, all of Athens was extremely worried for Harriet. We felt she was listening to a syren's song and heading for trouble and woe. On the other hand, one did not have to leave home for parts unknown to early seek the grave; just ask Aschah. Death was always just around the bend in the 19th century; no matter one's station nor location. Harriet did get to satisfy some of her dreams. She saw a part of this country in its then raw state before it was settled and populated. She experienced the virgin territory as few people ever had.

Have you determined what I meant by, "The glittering, treacherous bait?" Two things drove Harriet to leave Athens, one glittering, the other treacherous. The first was the glitter of Emanuel's promised wedding band. The second was the treacherous nature of the West. Harriet could resist neither.

To My Sister

Sister - I might not stain a leaf
In this dear book of thine,
Or trespass on thy time, ere brief -
With sentiment of mine;

Nor yet pay the sage of time
Or seek advise to give,
But that we part, to meet again,
Perhaps, not while we live.

Sister - the brightness and the bloom of youth
Sit joyous on thy brow
And candor, innocence and truth
Are inherent virtues now,
The world, to thy young guileless mind,
Seems beautiful and fair;
Nor would thy keenest searchings find
Deceit or baseness there.

Thus listen to its syren songs,
Credit its treacherous smiles,
Dwells one the flattery of its toungues
And revels mid its wiles.
Thou hast not dream'd guilt lurks beneath
A covering so fair,
Or what the slanderer's deadly breath
Rides on so pure as air

Sister - hath seen the songster gay
Play round the hunter's square,
Nor think of dangers in its way,
Till its death shriek rend the air?
And hast thou felt the tear spring forth
Unbidden to thine eye
To see such innocence and mirth
Thus treacherously die?

Its ease is thine - no more secure
Thy present happy state;
No more thy power to endure
The glittering, treacherous bait.
To often Friendship's holy name,
Assists to spread the snare,
While hatred, malise, envy reigns
(in demons glory there)

How oft does pleasure's winning smiles
Direct to ruins tend,
And often fancied joy beguiles
Its notaries to their ends.
A thousand solemn days nice divide
To entrap the virtous heart,
And oft the truly good and wise
Fall victim to its art

But though such perils set thy path
Let virtue be thy guide -
Smile at the wiley tempter's wraths,
And scorn the world beside.
Live with an eye to honor here,
To happiness and love;
And earnest seek that peace so dear,
A glorious rest above!

A tribute of esteem
from your brother
John Brough

♦ ♦ ♦ ♦

Goldsmith: My poem to Harriet was intended to remind her that her sincere good nature was being squandered on that undeserving young man. She belonged with a man of her own class and background, not this commoner. I ranked him with the worthless of the world. Frankly, it was my opinion that Miss Harriet fraternized with far too many people with whom she did not belong.

Good nature is a jewel well applied,
Bestowed where merit due observation claim.
But used without discrimination,
Without distinguishment of right or wrong,
It fools its own intent, and leaves no mark
Of good behind. E'en charity itself
Will lose its golden estimation, when
Exerted for the worthless and the vain

June 22nd 1834 Athens Ohio
(Goldsmith)

(Harriet must have disagreed with the author's conclusion as she erased his name from the page. Erasing ink was no simple matter in the 1830's, one used an instrument which looks much like a physician's scalpel to literally scrape away the ink whilst trying not to puncture the page.)

♦ ♦ ♦ ♦

Anonymous: In the tradition of commonplace books containing important time honored truths about the world I added these two well-known quotes which I transcribed from Athens second newspaper, *The Spectator*. It seems to me that they are as true today as they were back in the 1800's.

Learning is wealth to the poor, an honor to the rich,
And a support and comfort to the aged.

Friendship improves happiness and abates misery by the doubling of our joy and dividing of our grief.
Spectator

♦ ♦ ♦ ♦

Lucy M. Nye: In 1835 I lived with my mother, Lydia, in Dover Township, north of Athens. As you can see from my poem to Harriet, she was also my friend. I wrote her this poem, which has many common themes with others in her album: the fleeting nature of earthly pleasures, regret at her leaving, hope that we would meet again in heaven, and acknowledging that change was something that most people tried their best to avoid. It often meant the loss of someone close, as was the case with Harriet. This was a lamentable event in my life, to lose this dear friend. But her destiny lay in the West and so their eventual elopement, though shocking, was no real surprise.

I love at twlights meek and pensive hour
Alone to seek some calm sequestered bower
Far from the giddy and the thoughtless throng
To meditate, - or sing my evening song
To riffle mem'rys rich and treasured store
And muse oer scenes that cant return no more

Ah! Then vivid Fancy's magic glass
The friends of early days before me pass
The long lamented dead the absent friend
The false - the chang'd once more before me bend
Whilst one by one by one the glowing rays of day
Fade in the west and swiftly melt away
Tis thus I think that earthly pleasures fade
Whilst withering grief like evening's somere shade

Throws over our brightest joys its darksome gloom
And nips the buds of hope before they bloom
And then I love to think though sorrow now
May twine there wreath of cypress round my brow

There is a brighter world beyond the tomb
A realm of peace where joys immortal bloom
A home of rest (where life's sad journey's or)
Where friends ne'er change and parting is no more

Dover March 9th 1835 Lucy M. Nye

(Lucy married Laurentius Weethee in Athens County February 25, 1836, Dover Township)

♦ ♦ ♦ ♦

E.P. Pratt: I entered my poem on the same day that Aschah Pruden entered her poem, *The Rose.* She was, by that point, Mrs. John Brough. My name is Eliphaz Perkins Pratt, most people just call me EP. Became a clergyman I did, after I graduated from Ohio University, in 1837. I was in Athens and a witness to the elopement of Harriet and her beau and the subsequent removal of Silas and Mary from Athens in 1837.

I did not know Harriet as well as others in her album but was invited to inscribe a poem. I chose this one, which I had recently written. It in part describes how quaint and picturesque Athens was back in those days. I thought it would help Harriet to envision her hometown, in later years, when she might review these lines. The Hocking is the river which flows through Athens.

Sonnet - to the Moon

On Hocking's bosom, as he calmly flows,
And his cool aroma around our village throws,

Through classic vale, rolling this crystal tide,
Begist with thickest groves on either side,
How calmly sleep thy beams mild queen of night!
How peaceful rest thy rays of silver light!
How mild thy empire, O fair virgin queen!
How dark the forest shade! How still the scene!
Thus hid by thy silver septre, zephyrs sleep,
On dewy leaves that overhang the deep.
Nor dare to whisper through the boughs, nor stir
The valley's willows, nor the mountains far.
Nor make the pale and breathless poppie quiver
Nor brush, with ruffling wing, our glassy river.

Feb. 8th 1836 E.P. Pratt

♦ ♦ ♦ ♦

Maria F. Pratt: I wrote my poem to Harriet about a month after my brother (E.P. Pratt). Harriet and I had been discussing heaven, and though she was a good Christian, she believed that one could find heaven on earth. Life was so short, difficult and uncertain back in the 1830's that few people agreed with her. I hoped, for Harriet's sake, she was right. Our common belief was that true happiness, security and ease were not things of this world but of the next. Knowing that she was heading into "the stormy flood" of being a settler, I assumed life would be getting much more difficult for her there. Fearing the worst, I wished her peace and happiness in the hereafter.

"But there is a heaven for the good,
Far far beyond the stormy flood;
More peaceful than the sunny lake,
When nothing doth its surface break;
More calm than summer evenings are,
More glorious than the morning star.
And the blest souls who enter there,
And breathe that pure and heavenly air,

The more secure from all alarms
Than infants in their Mother's arms,
May this blest heaven then be thine;
And this I know can be;
May'st thou inherit joys divine;
'Tis all I ask for thee."

Maria F. Pratt Athens March 1836

♦ ♦ ♦ ♦

Ann C.C. Starr: Ann Catherine Clayton Starr is my name. It still brings a tear to my eye, all these years later, thinking about that lovely lass Harriet and her true love, Emanuel. It was my honor to write in Harriet's shrine. She was such a determined young woman, so full of ambition and imagination. She was the kind of person that collected true friends effortlessly through her sincere good works. One couldn't help but love her. I wrote this just before they stole away to Logan to get married.

So you know, I descend from Irish immigrants. My family lived east of Athens and close to Prudensville.

When the years have rolled o'er thee,
And summers are fled
And this comes before thee,
Like one from the dead,
When these scenes and these days
Shall be past and afar,
Let them live in the blaze
Of bright Memory's star

Then when friends long departed
Before thee appear,
And the gay and warm hearted
In fancy are near,
When all fond things together their

Remembrance shall bring,
For me let one feather
Be plucked from her wing

A.C.C. Starr June 28 1836

♦ ♦ ♦ ♦

Ann C.C. Starr: When I wrote this poem to Harriet, back in 1836, the Territories were thought of as a vast uncharted ocean which simply swallowed up so many poor souls. Many people who ventured forth were never seen or heard from again. Most came to some terrible end; if the Indians didn't get you, there were a hundred other ways to find an untimely and often violent death. When Harriet and Emanuel left I was keenly worried about her. She was not made for that difficult life. I could only echo previous poets in saying I hoped we would meet again, to part no more when, after life's toils, we met "beyond the skies."

Thoughts on Parting

When will parting scenes be over?
Separation known no more,
When will friendship bloom again,
Love and bliss forever reign?
When mortality is over,
Then will parting be no more -
When misfortune's weary blast
Blights the pleasures of the past;
When no gleam of joy I see,
Memory then returns to thee
Days departed I review
Scenes of pleasure spent with you
When will separation erase -
Friendships sons unite in peace -
Grief no more opposes the heart -

When the scenes of life are over,
Friends will meet to part no more.
When thy virtue I review,
Joys departed spent with you,
Hope renews the pleasing strain
Surely we shall meet again!
Yes when this frail body dies,
We shall meet beyond the skies

A.C.C. Starr

(Ann CC Starr was born in 1811 and died June 4, 1839, at twenty-eight years old. She was married to Thomas Welch on June 1, 1837 in Athens.)

♦ ♦ ♦ ♦

Anonymous: My poem needs little explanation. Harriet was everything I say she was. I was the Librarian at Ohio University back in those days. I would see Miss Pruden in town, at church, or at other social functions where we would have delightful discussions on a wide range of topics. She was especially interested in anything having to do with the Far West. I adored Harriet, much as everyone else in Athens did. A muse is defined as "the Goddess or the power regarded as inspiring a poet." The proof that Harriet was our muse is this old album itself and the many poems within, all inspired by this young woman. I did not sign my name to the poem because I did not want my wife to know that I was in love with another woman, even if purely a platonic love. My wife was a jealous woman.

To Miss Harriet

"Oh, there are many to be loved,
Few to be loved as thou,

Few to be thought of when away,
As thou are thought of now.

That lingering softness which some leave
Like twilight round the heart,
Which makes their name a charm to us
Long after they depart.

Those to whose thought such sacredness,
Such holy power is given
The love we feel for them on earth
Is like the love of Heaven,

God bless thou, gentle, heavenly friend;
And when life's storms shall cease,
May'st thou, u precious pearl, be cast
On the bright shores of peace."

Ohio University March 19th Inscribed by a friend

♦ ♦ ♦ ♦

C.B: This is a saying passed down in my family. Many of we 19th century Americans believed that one's faith and chances for happiness were inextricably linked. Was Harriet holy? Was she happy? One can gather from seeing her through the eyes of so many others that the girl was practically a saint. So yes, I would say she was holy, and thus happy and content. We can all learn a thing or two from her example.

"If you would be happy you must be
Holy - for happiness and holiness are
Inseparable." C.B.

Chapter Two

Logan, Ohio & Indiana 1837 to 1852

Emanuel Light: Finally, after one hundred and seventy some odd years I can set the record straight! *I tried talking Harriet out of going west.* Even I felt it would be too hard on her. That is one of the reasons we remained in Athens for six years after the commencement of her album.

I might as well start at the beginning. I first met Miss Harriet Pruden while doing work for her father. My brother, Josiah, and I were carpenters and worked all over Logan and Athens Counties. We did rough framing, finish carpentry and built cabinets. In this case we were working on a new barn. Mr. Pruden gave us lodging in an old cabin and board while the work proceeded.

Harriet and her siblings would come around to check on the work, sometimes Harriet would bring us our dinner and we would talk. Harriet immediately caught my eye and I was amazed to come to the conclusion that she seemed to be flirting with me. Why a wealthy young lady of such obvious class would have any interest in a poor carpenter was beyond me. Well, not entirely, in my youth I was a handsome rascal, and a charmer with the ladies. I remember thinking, why not play along a little while? What could it hurt?

Harriet was exceedingly attractive and, as I came to find out, exceedingly ambitious. Not for wealth or power but for knowledge and adventure. Harriet had the desire to see the

West. Her favorite stories were of Lewis and Clark. She had memorized most of the Indian tribes on that venture and could recite volumes of information on each one. She longed to see the many animals and plants, not known in Ohio, but described by the early explorers. She wanted to swim in the Pacific Ocean. I told her about my brother 'P' and his wife Elizabeth, who were shortly to strike out for northern Indiana, then the home of many well-armed Indians. I was no stranger to hard work nor to living in the woods and was toying with the idea of joining my relations there, when and if I could afford to outfit myself. It was the only way a poor man like me would ever be able to obtain my own land and so I was working and saving my wages as best as I was able. Harriet said, "It isn't exactly west, but it is definitely the wilderness!" I wanted to head west for the opportunity, Harriet for the adventure. She saw the big picture better than I and taught me how this was a historical opportunity that would never again be possible. She was ahead of her time when she predicted the West would be won and settled in less than a century -she was right!

People in Athens came to call me "the Syren's Song," meaning that I was sweetly tempting an innocent Harriet down a path which would lead her into misery. The fact of the matter is that Harriet was the Syren's Song to me. I might never have gone to Indiana had it not been for Harriet's seductive powers of persuasion. She eventually convinced me it was the right thing to do, an opportunity of a lifetime, and sold me on her romantic dream. I may have been the catalyst but it was Harriet that set the whole thing in motion.

In those days, for a young lady of means and advantage to be seen with someone of my lower status, for anything other than business, was a taboo. Men like myself did not, could not, have social interests in such a woman without stirring up a hornet's nest. Most other girls in Harriet's position listened to their parents without question. Harriet was the exception to this rule. She had a reputation for befriending anyone she felt was an honest person of good character, no matter their station in life. She freely came and went around Athens visiting with all her friends, rich and poor, men and women.

She also had a weakness for underdogs, and hence was a strong supporter of the abolition movement.

As it turned out, we had common interests other than the desire to be a part of our country's expansion. We both enjoyed reading poetry. We both felt like it was possible to find heaven on earth, not a popular thought at the time. I have my own mother to thank for my love of verse. She made sure all the children knew how to read and write. She also instructed us in manners. We were poor but proud. My brothers often kidded me because I spent so much time trying to write poetry. They thought it a pastime exclusively of the rich.

Harriet was impressed that I could quote from well-known modern poets (they were modern then) and we became friends. She loaned me books and brought the latest news of the West. We would recite and discuss the latest poems, which she found in magazines and newspapers. We did not work on Sunday and after church I was on occasion invited to join Harriet and her sister, Aschah, on walks or horseback rides. Of course romantic notions crossed my mind. Harriet was truly a delight to the eye but I never would have dared act on those notions, it just was not done.

In this matter Harriet would take the lead. One Sunday she claimed to not feel well and so her family went off to an all day church affair leaving her in Maxon's care. As soon as they left she came and got me for a walk in the woods. I took her hand crossing a creek but she did not let go after we crossed, so we walked along hand in hand. As we proceeded I spied a fawn lying totally still and quiet in a nearby thicket. The fawn was very close but Harriet did not see it, it was well camouflaged. I stood behind Harriet and pointed it out over her shoulder. Standing so close I felt her warmth. My God, she smelled good! Slowly she turned to face me and we gazed deeply into each other's eyes. It seemed so natural, so effortless and we melted together and kissed ever so softly.

So began our secret love affair. We thought we were being so discreet, sneaking off to the woods to be alone together. We passed notes at secret drops. We had our prearranged rendezvous and thought we were fooling everyone. Harriet continued to be courted by many a suitor, arranged by her mother. She kept up the illusion that everything was normal. Mary Pruden invited a constant stream of promising young men from the local university to various social functions at the Pruden household. She had six daughters to marry off, after all, and had convinced most of the professors at Ohio University to help her do so by bringing young men they approved of by the house. Harriet truly liked many of these gentlemen but never seriously considered any for a husband. They were all home-bodies who would never help her achieve her goal of living in the Far West.

Eventually the barn project was finished. My brother and I were able to find other work in and around Athens. When we were finished with his project but still working in the area, Silas Pruden allowed us to let the little cabin and provided us with our evening meal for a reasonable rate. My brother knew the depth of feeling between Harriet and me. He said we would be lucky to escape being tarred and feathered and run out of town. He pleaded with me to give her up. "It will never work out Emanuel. She is refined and you will never be able to support her in the grand style she is accustomed to," he would say, then would add, "even if you and she did marry and head west how long do you think it would be before she tired of all the toil of a settler's life and called it quits?" All valid points, I conceded. When I discussed these same points with Harriet she assured me that she understood the danger and was not afraid of hard work.

By the winter of 1830 we had exhausted our workload in Athens and so had no choice but to return to Logan. I continued to communicate with Harriet by sending her letters. I sent them to her friend Ann Maxon (she was in the Pruden's employ) who would see that they discreetly reached Harriet.

Up until late that winter only Maxon and Josiah knew about the two of us. Then Harriet let the cat out of the bag. She announced (!) to her family that she was going to accept my offer of marriage and would accompany me into the wilderness. The word spread like wildfire in the small town, and I for one was glad I was not around in that moment when tempers and emotions were running so high. I very well might have ended up tarred and feathered! I was unable to return to

Athens until well into the following spring but return I did. It was time for me to make my own stand and see if I could convince the Pruden family to accept me, to accept us as a couple. Josiah declined my invitation to accompany me back to Athens. He said he would prefer to read about the lynching in the newspaper.

It was providential for me that I had been befriended the previous year not only by Silas Pruden but also by Archibald G. Brown. They complimented my skills during the building of the barn. Both genuinely liked me. They were at least somewhat impressed that I had both manners and was well-read, despite my lack of formal education. Further, both sympathized with my predicament. Both understood Harriet was an irresistible creature who could easily bend the will of even the hardest man. Mr. Pruden said that if I got a proper job and could convince Harriet it was foolishness, this becoming settlers, he thought eventually I would be accepted as a suitable mate for their beloved daughter.

Thus began six hard years of my attempts at becoming a gentleman, as well as trying to convince Harriet to at least delay the adventure west. I failed on both counts. First, I relished being my own master too much; I just couldn't work under someone else. Second, Harriet adamantly refused to marry me until I took her away from Athens and we began our 'adventure.' Third, it became more and more apparent that the harder I tried to be accepted, the more Mrs. Pruden despised me. There was only so much groveling I could stomach. It eventually became clear that it just was not going to work for us in Athens and so we eloped.

Our adventure began in a creaky old wagon drawn by a pair of white socked bays. Heading northwest, we traveled up the Hocking River Valley as it meanders through the hills and deep, lush forests, as far as Logan, Ohio, where we married December 7, 1837. Our first child, David, was born there in 1839. By 1840 we had made it to our new home in Elkhart County, in far northern Indiana. Believe you me, in those times it was the Wild West!

I wrote the following poem to my own true love, Harriet, a few months before we married.

Man is the rugged lofty pine
That frowns on many a wave beat shore
Woman, the slender graceful vine
Whose curling tendril round it twines
And deck its rough bark sweetly ore

Man is the rock whose hovering crest
Nods on the mountains barren side
Woman the soft and mossy vest
That loves to clasp its steril brest
And wreath its brow in vardent pride

Man is the cloud of coming storm
Dark as the ravens murky plume
Gave where the sunbeam bright and near
Of womans soul and womans form
Gleams brightly ore the gathering gloom

Yes lovely sex to you is given
To rule our hearts with angle sway
Blend with each no (*know*) a blissful heaven
Change erth into a perfect heaven
And sweetly smile our cares away

March 20, 1837   ESL *(Emanuel Light)*

♦ ♦ ♦ ♦

James R. Wert: The Battle of the Alamo and San Jacinto was just one year before I wrote this poem to Harriet. A few of us heard they were in need of men for the militia and so were heading south to the Republic of Texas (Texas didn't become a state until 1845).

The worst part of leaving was saying goodbye to Miss Harriet Pruden, soon to be, Mrs. Light. I was good friends with Emanuel but totally smitten with his fiancé, so until they said their vows she was fair game for a little impromptu flirting.

Emanuel was very understanding. He had nothing to worry about. Her heart was only for him and he knew it. Besides he could have whipped any of his competition. Not that he was a brawler, but he was big, strong and agile as a cat. So, I wrote this poem to an engaging young lady that stole my heart. I knew I had no chance of ever being any more than her friend.

Oh, hush the soft sigh, avail, and dry the sweet tear
To this bosom thy image shall ever be dear;
Of hope's pictured scenes how the colors decay,
And love's fairy season as soon melts away!

When its balm breathing dew I delighted to sip,
Did I think a farewell would escape from that lip
By honor commands though far should I roam
The loadstone of love will attract me to home.

Logan March 9th 1837 James R. Wert

♦ ♦ ♦ ♦

Mary Hildreth: My father had business in Logan and I went with him to see Harriet. I had collected this poem out of a newspaper shortly after Harriet left Athens and I thought of her when I read it. I was very worried for her. They would soon be leaving for the wild woods. I believed that even if things did go badly for Harriet Light (they were by now married), there would be rest in heaven for my friend. It was our belief that the only constant in life was faith in the afterlife.

We had a wonderful but short visit. We gossiped. I told her the news from Athens, how everyone was faring. Her parents had also moved to Hocking County, they say because Mrs. Pruden was embarrassed about her daughter's elopement. Some suspected Harriet was in a motherly way when she left Athens, which was pure gossip. She missed her friends and family but was excited that they were finally to begin their western adventure.

I was glad that I had seen Harriet again and had the opportunity to record this poem in her album. I hope it brought her comfort in her days in the wild. It would be the last time I ever saw her.

To Miss H.....P.......

Should sorrow o'er thy brow
Its darkened shadows fling,
And hopes that cheer thee now
Die in their early spring -
Should pleasure at its birth
Fade like the hues of even
Turn thou away from earth,
Theres rest for thee in heaven.

If ever life shall seem
To thee a toilsome way
And gladness cease to beam
Upon its clouded day -
If like the weary dove
O'er shoreless oceans driven
Raise thou thine eye above
Theres rest for thee (*in*) heaven
But oh! If thornless flowers
Throughout thy pathway bloom
And gaily fleet the hours
Unstained by earthly gloom;
Still let not every thought
To this poor world be given
Not always be forgot
Thy better rest in heaven

Transcribed by your friend   Mary Hildreth

♦ ♦ ♦ ♦

Mary Cleveland: I met Harriet in Logan in 1838 during Martin van Buren's presidency. She was still a newlywed and was very happy –at first anyway. Her marriage had tempered the loss of her sister Aschah, but this year would bring twice the misery with the loss of not just her mother but also of her sister Rebecca.

Harriet and I met at church and became fast friends. She and her husband, Emanuel, were working and saving money to outfit themselves for their planned trip to the wilderness of Northern Indiana.

O may thy angel true
The chain of life extend
And add a thousand links thereto
To praise thee merry friend

Bright beams attend the gentle one
The kindest and the best
For sorrow scarse can fall upon
A heart so truly blest

Mary Cleveland

♦ ♦ ♦ ♦

Ann E. Busking: Harriet and Emanuel were a fine young couple and their benevolent nature was well known in Logan. However, they believed they could find a heaven on earth and were bound and determined to seek their happiness in the wilderness, where, as they said, their hearts commanded them to go. What scared many of us was alluringly attractive to the young couple.

I added this poem because none of the others even mentioned the Bible. It was a rock of security that most clung to in our uncertain lives. Yes, I suppose I was proselytizing a bit, but then I do come from an evangelical family, we were supposed to spread the word. I wanted the young couple to remember that the Bible would offer them security and comfort if their dreams let them down or if they found themselves lost in the wilderness. Mine was possibly the last poem entered from Logan. They left for northern Indiana less than a week later.

The Bible

"What is the world? A wildering maze
Where sin has tracked ten thousand ways,
Her victims to ensnare
All broad and winding and a slope,
All tempting with perfidious hope,
All ending in despair.

Millions of pilgrims throng the roads,
Bearing their bauble, or their bags
Down to eternal night,
One humble path that never bends,
Narrow, and rough, and steep, ascends
From darkness into light

Is there no guide to show that path?
The Bible - he alone that hath
The Bible need not stray;
Yet he who hath and will not give
That light of life to all who live,
Himself shall lose the way."

Logan Febua. 2nd 1840 Ann E. busking

(This poem is also in Rebecca's album [see pages 16 and 129], though dated from 1830. It must have been published somewhere but that source has since been lost)

♦ ♦ ♦ ♦

Phebe Martin: Aside from Harriet's only two pieces, mine was the first poem from northern Indiana entered into her album. She and Emanuel had arrived there a few months before. It was only two short years after the majority of the natives were forcibly evicted from those same lands. The young Light family joined us in Middlebury on the banks of the Little Elkhart River. Middlebury could by only a hair's breadth be called a town then, with a mere twelve settler families as its entire population. Harriet and I met at our little canvas covered church and quickly became fast friends. What an astonishing woman she was. Harriet had given up the good life that most of us would never know to pursue her dreams and her love. She had given up fine clothes, a large home with servants, fancy parties, and a secure future to come and take her chances with us in the wilderness. To everyone's amazement she fit right in and became a joy to us all.

When I read this poem by Fredrich Adolf Krummacher (1767-1845) I knew that he was speaking of our Harriet. Indeed she was "the fairest found where all is fair." and like the subject of the poem, was now clothed in simple garb. But even "clothed in Nature's simplest weed," there was still no other who could match Harriet's looks or kind-hearted demeanor and she became our treasure, our very own 'Moss Rose.'

The Moss Rose

The angel of the flower and day
Beneath a rose tree sleeping lay
That spirit to whose charge is given
To bathe young buds in dew from heaven
Awakening from its light repose
The angel whispered to the rose
O choicest object of my care
Still fairest found where all is fair
For the sweet shade thou'st given to me
Ask what you wilt tis granted thee
Then said the rose with deepened glow
On me another grace bestow?
The spirit pawed in silent thought

What grace was there the flower had not?
Twas but a moment o'er the rose
A vail of moss the angel throws
And clothed in Nature's simplest weed
Could there a flower that rose exceed?

June 21 1840 Phebe Martin

♦ ♦ ♦ ♦

Harriet (Pruden) Light: Well, you have been hearing *about* me for a long time, now I suppose it is time you heard *from* me. First, let me say that I have no regrets about my decision to become Mrs. Emanuel Light. Certainly I had second thoughts during those six years we stayed in Athens. The present of my poetry album was so incredibly touching, it accomplished what its intention was, to illustrate how many true friends I had at home. I was deeply moved and very grateful. Emanuel thought we could make a go of it in Ohio so we put off our plans for heading west. However, he was never truly accepted there and neither of us could get the wanderlust out of our system.

I knew life in the West would be fraught with danger; I was not as naive or innocent as people thought, but we had to go. We had to see the unspoiled sights before they were gone, it would not last long in its pristine state. We were some of the first to go but I was sure it would not be long before we would be followed by countless others. There just wasn't any land left in the East. The wilderness was magnificent, wild and untamed, I wouldn't have missed it for the world. My only two poetic entries in this endearing old album were entered shortly after we arrived in that brand new world. I loved my commonplace book but relied mainly on others to fill it. I never was much of a poet.

I missed my friends and family terribly after we left, but I had my poetry album and so would visit with them there. I was sorry that I had so embarrassed my parents that they felt it necessary to move away from Athens. My mother, rest her soul, simply had other dreams for me than those I chose for myself. "To thine own self be true," as Mr. Shakespeare said.

Life in Indiana was extremely difficult. As Mary Perkins predicted in her poem to me, I did indeed find myself "in toils, in countless round," but for me it was a labor of love and I did my work happily. Education for the young ones was in short supply in the wilderness and I found that I was able to help out there by teaching reading and writing once a week. One of our few textbooks was my poetry album. I was quite surprised by how the children took to it, even the boys rarely missed a class.

I did grow melancholy at times for easier days, especially during the harsh Indiana winters. I missed my hometown and my mother, and I missed Aschah and Rebecca, who both died so young. When I came across this poem it was as if it had been written by me or at least about me. It wasn't, of course, but might as well have been. I had much in common with it's author, Laura M. Thurston (aka Viola). We were both the same age, give or take a year and we both had come west to Indiana. Likewise, Laura mentions how much she missed her home land when she says, "vanished is the beacon light that cheered my morning sky!" I always thought of my sisters when reading that line. Also, Laura's description of her home reminded me so much of dear old Athens, Ohio.

It might seem to you, after reading my only two entries, that this young woman you have come to know through others' words as an explorer and forward looking woman was now tamed and looking back in regret. The truth is I was always positive about the future; I had great hopes for a bright one. That is until a month or so before Eugene's birth. The hard life had beaten me down after three years of constant toil. I suppose my upbringing did not prepare me for this lifestyle. In that, my old friends from Ohio were right. The winter of 1843 was horribly cold and we were trapped in the cabin for the most part. Our provisions were thinning and I did not have enough food for a pregnant woman. I contracted a high fever from a chest cold and in my weakened state the fever ravaged me. It was then that I knew my adventure was almost over. Still, I was determined to deliver this child first. I hoped I would live on through my children and that they would carry on with the adventure. They did not let me down.

(Harriet would die giving birth to her son, Eugene, November 22, 1843. She was only twenty-eight. She is buried south of Middlebury, Indiana in Forest Grove Cemetery. The baby survived. Like Harriet, the poet Laura Thurston also died young in Indiana, in 1842.)

The Green Hills of my Father's Land

The green hills of my Father's land
In dreams still greet my view;
The sky - the glorious sky, outspread
Above their calm repose -
The river, oer its rocky bed
Still singing as it flows -
The stillness of the Sabbath hours,
When men go up to pray -
The sunlight resting on the flowers -
The birds that sing among the bowers,
Thro' all the summer day.

Land of my birth! Mine early love!
Once more thine air I breathe!
I see thy proud hills tower above -
Thy green vales sleep beneath
Thy groves shy rocks thy murmuring riles
All rise before mine eyes
The dawn of morning on thy hills
Thy gorgeous sunset skies -
Thy forests from whose deep recess
A thousand streams have birth
Glad'ning the lonely wilderness
And filling the green silentness
With melody and mirth

I wonder if my home would seem
As lovely as of youre!

I wonder if the mountain stream
Goes singing by the door!
And if the flowers still bloom as fair
And if the woodlines climb
As when I used to train them there
For the dear olden time
I wonder if the birds still sing
Upon the garden tree
As sweetly as in that sweet spring
Whose gentle memory doth bring
So many dreams to me!

I know that there hath been a chang(*e*)
A change o'er hall and hearth!
Faces and footsteps new and strange
About my place of birth
The heavens above are still as bright
As in the gone by
But vanished is the beacon light
That cheered my morning sky!
The hill and vale and wooden glen
The rock and murmuring stream
That were such glorious beauty then
Would seem should I return again
The record of a dreem

I mourn not for my childhood's hours
Since in the far off west
Neath sunnier skies in greener bowery
My heart hath found its rest
I mourn not for the hills and streams
That claim'd my steps so long
Yet still I see them in my dreams,
And hail them in my song;

And often by the hearth fire's blaze,
When winter's eve's shall come,
We'll sit and talk of other days

And sing the well remembered lays
Of my green mountain home

March 2, 1840 Harriet Light

♦ ♦ ♦ ♦

Anonymous: I wrote a simple poem expressing how we treasure our children for their innocence and beauty. Not much has changed on that subject in the one hundred and seventy-five years since. Olivia, in her poem *The Three Homes* says that children live in such innocence that, "every world is joy and truth/and treasures live in flowers." How can one not cherish such little darlings?

Life was not easy for the family after Harriet's death but they carried on. Many an evening, around the hearth, Emanuel would read from the Remembrance Album to the growing boys. He read these poems which speak of their mother's beauty and fine character. As there were no official schools yet established in Elkhart County, David and Eugene got their first schooling learning to read and copy the poetry in the album.

Fairest and Best

There came a child to my side one day,
And lightly she said with a laugh of mirth,
Tell me of all things, now I pray,
Which is the fairest to you upon earth?
Is it the rose, with its breath of balm?
Is it the gem of the diamond mine?
Is it the shell, with its sea song calm?
Or the pearl, that lone in the deep doth shine?
I answered her. Though the rose is fair,
Though the diamond gleams like a lesser sun;
Oh ne'er can thee, e'en in thought compare,
With my chosen beauty, my present one.

♦ ♦ ♦ ♦

Harriet (Pruden) Light: As I mentioned before, because both of my poems look back to former times you might be of the opinion that I was regretting my decision to head west. Yes I missed many things from my days in Ohio, but I never regretted my decision. I had true love with Emanuel, we had a fine family and many dear friends. We had a grand adventure and saw things few before us had. I got to be the explorer I always wanted to be; maybe not another Lewis or Clark, but for a woman in that day and age, I blazed a few trails. The only regret I have is that I was not able to venture down a few more.

Memory

How sweet to sigh o'er joys gone by,
O'er friends that now have ceas'd to be,
O'er happy hours in moonlight bow'rs,
When once recalled by Memory.

How oft upon the sunny green,
Has pleasure beam'd from every eye!
Ah, who would drown in Lethean stream
The pleasures of sweet Memory!

March 23 1840 H.L.

♦ ♦ ♦ ♦

Harriet (Pruden) Light: I wrote this marker in my album shortly after we arrived in Elkhart County, Indiana, in 1840. I was sitting watching David and Brice play together and wanted David to remember who his first friend was in our new home in the wilderness, and to remember where that home was. Brice was already a young man then, David was still a little fellow, less than two. I hoped David might recall this period in his life whenever he might be reading from our commonplace book. I was so excited to finally be there, to be a part of westward expansion and to be one of the very first settlers to *ever* see this land. I felt I was a part of history.

David M. Light
Brice Larimer
Little Elkhart - Elkhart County, Indiana

♦ ♦ ♦ ♦

NOBODY!: I came from the East Coast to Indiana at about the same time as the Light family. I was in search of adventure and hoped to make my fortune, but that was not to be. My blood was poisoned from a hunting wound and I died in my youth without realizing my dreams. Mrs. Light helped out when I was on my deathbed. She would come calling, her child in tow, and bring food and other provisions. After tidying up my pathetic little cabin she would visit with me, including reading from her poetry album. The Lights basically adopted me as I was one of the few in the area who did not have a family. I was well educated back east and was familiar with and fond of poetry and literature in general. Mrs. Light and I often had conversations about such things. I asked if I could make a contribution to her album and she agreed. It would be my epitaph.

I chose a portion of Lord Byron's *Childe Harold*, 3rd canto, from the section titled *The Poet's Impulse, XCV11*. It is about Byron's struggle with finding the poet's perfect expression. That is not what it meant to me, lying there as I was on my deathbed. To me it represented my frustration over dying before I had even begun to pursue my dreams or achieve my goals. I signed it "NOBODY!" as I had not yet, and never would, have the chance to become somebody. The fickle finger of fate had seen to that. I suspect Harriet felt exactly the same way, but a short time later, when her time came to leave this world. Many of us died so terribly young in those days.

Could I embody all my bosom now;
That which is most within me - could I wreak
My thoughts upon expulsion & then throw
And, heart, mind, passions strange & weak,
All that I would have sought, & all I seek
Bear, know, feel & get breath into one word
And that word were Lightning, I would spark
But as it is, I live and die unheard,
With a most voiceless thought sheathing it as a sword

Inscribed by - **NOBODY!**

♦ ♦ ♦ ♦

'P': I am Emanuel's older brother. We moved from Virginia to Logan, Ohio when we boys were still young. My wife, Elizabeth, and I migrated to Elkhart County in 1835. It was four years before Emanuel and Harriet arrived there and before the federal government forcibly removed the native inhabitants, the Potowatami Indians. My family was befriended by the Indians and they taught us much about survival in the wilderness. I thought it an unforgivable travesty what we white people later did to our native friends. Most people did not distinguish between the many Indian tribes back then; they lumped them all together as savages. Nothing could be farther from the truth, just like with white men, there are good and bad Indians.

Emanuel and I were both lucky when it came to affairs of the heart. We both married women who truly loved us and inspired us to be our best. Both my Elizabeth and Emanuel's Harriet taught us the joys of love. I wrote this poem in tribute to the fairer sex in general, and to Elizabeth and Harriet in particular.

Woman's Love

There is a feeling in the heart,
A thought within the bosom's swell
Which Woman's eyes alone impart;
Which Woman's blush alone can tell!

Man may be cold in love's disguise
And feel not half the flame he speaks
But Woman's love is in her eyes;
It glows upon her burning cheeks!

P.

♦ ♦ ♦ ♦

Anonymous: All of us boys in Elkhart had huge crushes on Mrs. Harriet Light. So naturally when she offered to help with the schooling of us youngsters by reading and teaching us the poetry in her book, we all wanted to attend, whether we liked poetry or not. There were at that time no real schools in Elkhart County. I found that I actually enjoyed poetry and would clamor for any scrap of reading material I could get my hands on. There were very few books around then, which is why Mrs. Light's was considered such a treasure. We did occasionally get an old newspaper or magazine from other settlers passing through.

That was where I got this poem, or piece of a poem. I couldn't have been more than twelve years of age at the time. It is actually only one of seven verses of a piece by Sarah Roberts Boyle (1812-1869) which I knew was not in Mrs. Light's album. It is one of the few poems from my times still popular today. I brought the poem to our class and recited this one verse to the other children. Mrs. Light said she was so impressed that she wanted me to write it in her album. Now understand, we kids never even got to hold the album, for fear of spilling something on it or otherwise damaging it. So it was with fear and trepidation that I set about making my contribution. As you can see by my handwriting I was not yet a competent writer and Mrs. Light suggested I write in pencil so I could easily correct any mistakes I might make. She also had me practice writing the poem on other bits of paper before I did my final version in her book. I still managed to make a few mistakes. Mrs. Light seemed nonetheless genuinely pleased with my contribution. I received a big hug for my effort which flustered me. I blushed beet red for a full week, much to my embarrassment and everyone else's delight.

The Voice of the Grass

here I come creeping creeping every
where. you can not see me coming,
nor heare my low sweet humming
far in the starry night and the glad
morning light I come quietly creeping
every where -

Spring

♦ ♦ ♦ ♦

L.C. Sanger: Lucas Sanger here. I knew Harriet and Emanuel from Indiana. Like virtually everyone in Indiana at that time, my family and I were also settlers come from the East, Connecticut in our case. I was born in 1809 and my wife, Louisa, was born in 1819. My two daughters, Phebe and Laura, were not yet born when I wrote this poem to Mrs. Harriet Light, the Muse of Middlebury, Indiana.

We all knew of her poetry album. Next to her family it was her most precious possession. I wrote this poem in it to let her know that she defined true friendship as far as everyone in Elkhart County was concerned. You would be hard pressed to find a better example. To quote one of the other poets, she was indeed a "ministering angel from the skies."

Harriet was known for her benevolence. It was fitting that her last act was one of giving: she gave birth to her son. No one expected her to make it long enough to come to term, a weaker soul wouldn't have. Harriet had a big heart and refused to succumb until after the birth. God bless her.

To Mrs Harriet Light

Friendship

...The smiling earth on which we tread
Were but a desert found
Did not enlivening friendship shed
Its cheering influence round
The waving fields were but a mild
And shining skies above
Did not dear friends our care beguile
Would dark and cheerless prove

For friendship has to charm
The heart of those distressed
And sympathetic feelings warm
The soul by grief oppressed
When adverse winds of fortune blow
And brightest prospects fade
We find it easy then to know
The friends whom affluence made

Though many may pretend to love
We should not trust too far
It needs but little time to prove
Who fortune's followers are
They're those who when distress invade
And pleasure's changed to grief
Ne'er strive to raise the drooping head
Or timely give relief

But should we pass through sorrow's vale
Should clouds our sky obscure

And find those there when others fail
Who prove their friendship pure
We safely can in them confide
Nor need we ever fear
Whatever sorrow may betide
They'll ever prove sincere
With those who still my path surround
May I not number you
And let us make the happy choice
To sit at jesus's feet
To sing his praise unite our voice
Till round the throne we meet

When all our comforts fade and die
When youthful vigor's gone
There is a mansion in the sky
To which we're hastening on
And while we through this thorny maze
Our weary steps may wend
Until at last at length of days
We to the tomb descend

We have the sweet assurance still
Though friends inconstant rove
We've one above who never will
Or can unfaithful prove
And from his ever liberal hand
Our comforts all proceed
And till we reach that happy land
His merits we will plead

And when we find our long-sought home
And land on that bright shore
We shall no more in sorrow roam
Our grief and sin over
There dwells the object of our love
The friend of all mankind

We'll praise his glorious name above
With raptures unconfined

Middlebury Oct 25th, 1842 L.C. Sanger

♦ ♦ ♦ ♦

M Everts: I had spent the last year in the godforsaken wilderness of Northern Indiana when I wrote this poem to my Aunt Harriet, anticipating my departure the following spring. I was sick and tired of the constant toil and was going back to Ohio. I am the daughter of Harriet's sister Mary. My father Milo Everts and mother died very young, leaving my brother and me as orphans. We were passed around the family and I joined my aunt and her family here in Indiana in 1842 while my brother Lucien lived, for awhile, with John Brough.

The settlers here came to adore Harriet. Not only was she so kind-hearted and caring but they respected her courage for having given up the rich life to follow her husband into the wild. Emanuel's relatives here had spread the word that he was courting a socialite back in Ohio, so a spoiled brat was expected. Harriet surprised everyone. It wasn't long before they felt, rightly so, that even though she was a refined young woman she was not snobby or aloof. Instead, she fit right in. She was a hard worker and never complained about the constant toil that was a settler's lot. It was as if she had always been a settler's wife and before long no one could imagine life without Harriet. Unlike me, she never seemed to regret her circumstances.

This is one of the last poems ever written to her, she would die before the year was over. I did not know that when I wrote this, though she was sickly and pregnant at the time. This winter of '43 was just beginning. It would be the worst on record for many years after. Many settlers would perish in that terrible season.

It was left to me to carry the news home to Ohio that beloved Harriet had gone to join Grandmother Mary, Rebecca, Aschah, and all the other kinfolk in heaven.

To my Aunt Harriet

Dear aunt while memory remains
Though di(s)tant far my home may be
And should we neare meet again
I'll never forget thee
Should joy and peace my path surround
And life with sweet prosperity
In every time and place be crown'd
I'll never forget thee
Should grief and sorrow cloud my brow
And shades of dark adversity
Their gloom around my pathway throw
I'll never forget thee
But seek to find beyond this vale
This world of pain and misery
A friend who when all others fail
Will never forget thee!

Newbury (*Township, Indiana*) Sep 1 1843 M Everts

(Martha A. Everts returned from the West and lived with Harriet's brother David and his wife Elizabeth for the rest of her life. She too would die young in Sulphur Springs, Mississippi.)

♦ ♦ ♦ ♦

E.E.L.: I am Elizabeth (Bently) Light, second wife of Emanuel Light. I wrote this in Harriet's poetry album seven years after her death and three years after my marriage to Emanuel (in 1847). My poem was the first written in the album since her death and occurred the same year as William's birth, our first child. Harriet wanted her album to be passed down, she hoped it would be actively used by successive generations, as was the tradition with commonplace books. The album was almost buried along with Harriet as her most precious possession. Emanuel was persuaded to keep it as his only portrait of Harriet, a written portrait if you will (he had no drawing or painting of her and photography had not yet been invented). Emanuel also kept the album so the boys, both young at the time, could come to know their mother by reading and hearing the many poems which speak so fondly of her.

Harriet had been a good friend to me and my family while she lived. She was older than me by six years and I looked up to her as my counsel. We all grieved deeply after she passed. My parents also died young, just a year after Harriet, from the influenza, leaving just myself and two sisters. Emanuel and I each found ourselves in somewhat dire straits in the wilderness. We had become good friends and so gravitated towards each other for comfort and mutual support. Emanuel and I were not deeply in love when we married but we were good friends who needed each other. In time our love did grow. We lived a good life together and had a fine family of whom we were very proud.

In 1850 I thought it was high time we continued to collect new poetry in Harriet's album and so wrote and entered my poem. Its message had a twofold purpose, first to tell Emanuel how happy I felt we were and secondly as an apothegm for our children, to let them know what is really important in life...true friends.

Gentle Words

A young rose in summer time
Is beautiful to me,
And glorious the many stars
That glimmer on the sea;
But gentle words and loving hearts,
And hands to clasp my own,
Are better than the brightest flowers
Or stars that ever shown.
The sun may warm the grass to life,

The dew, the drooping flowers,
And eyes grow bright and watch the night
Of autum's opening hour -
But words that breathe of tenderness,
And smiles we know are true,
Are warmer than the summer time,
And brighter than the dew.

It is not much the world can give,
With all its subtle art,
And gold or gems are not the things
To satisfy the heart;
But oh! If those who cluster round
The altar and the hearth
Have gentle words and loving smiles,
How beautiful is earth!

Middlebury Feb 3 1850 E.E.L. (*Elizabeth Light*)

♦ ♦ ♦ ♦

Brice Larimer: My farewell wish to David was written in 1853 when the Light family was heading off to California during the Gold Rush. I had known David since he was just a small child and had always considered him my baby brother, though we were not actually related.

I first met David, Emanuel, and Harriet Light in 1840 when they moved to Elkhart County, Indiana. David was only one year old then so that made him fourteen when this was written. I took David under my wing during those years after Harriet died until Emanuel remarried to my wife's sister, Elizabeth. Those first years after Harriet's death were hard for Emanuel. He was grief-stricken and had two boys and a farm to manage, so I helped out the best I could. I would take David with me on hunting and fishing trips. When he was older I taught him to shoot, how to field dress animals, how to track. He was a quick learner and made both Emanuel and myself proud as he learned how to contribute to his family's provisioning.

I never heard from him after he left but did hear from Emanuel and Elizabeth after they reached the West. They said David had left them to try his hand at prospecting for gold. He had no luck and eventually hired on as a guide for emigrants, leading them through the Sierra Nevada Mountains and into California. They too lost track of him at that point and so no one knows what became of him. There was a rumor that he lost his life in a fight with Indians, but that was never confirmed.

To Mr. David Light

Where ere you go where ere you rove
May happiness be your lot

♦ ♦ ♦ ♦

Lucy E.(Bently) Larimer: I was born in New York State, in 1826. Emanuel's second wife, Elizabeth, was my older sister; Jane Bently was my younger sister. I wrote this poem to Jane upon the occasion of her departure for El Dorado in 1853. The Gold Rush was in full swing and Emanuel had convinced the family they would find a better life there. Unlike most folks, however, they were not heading west to mine for gold but to claim some of what was said to be incredibly fertile farmland. Emanuel was sick and tired of fighting the harsh Indiana winters and looked forward to the mild climate in the West. He and his first wife, Harriet, who had passed away back in 1843, had always wanted to see the Pacific Ocean, so he was keeping a promise to her posthumously.

I cannot remember exactly but I believe Millard Fillmore was then President of the States, or perhaps it was Franklin Pierce. What I do recall is that my nephew, Frank, was still just an infant when they left in their 'prairie schooner' as the wagons were called. Dear little William died on the trail, like so many did, from cholera. He was only four years old. For Emanuel and my sister losing their first-born child was a heavy blow. They loved him dearly. He lies buried somewhere along the California/Oregon Trail. Thank goodness everyone else made it safely through, we finally got word late the next year. There was no such thing as rapid communication back then so it was not unusual to wait long periods for word to reach us. As you can imagine it was very stressful, not knowing how loved one's were faring. It made one extremely anxious.

I married Brice Larimer in 1847, just a month or so after Emanuel and Elizabeth married, and we decided to stay in Indiana. We both wanted to see Elkhart County grow from the wilderness it was when we first arrived to be settled and populated with real towns, churches and schools. There we stayed for the rest of our lives. We had four children, three lived to be full grown.

My sister Jane and I were very close and I respected her kindness and selflessness. She reminded me of Harriet (who I had known well), very fetching and big hearted. Jane was known for her good deeds and work for others.

Friendships Wish

No rubies on the indian shore
Outshine thy noble mind
Its radiance far excels them all
And blesses humankind

A heart of heavenly purity
Is laid within thy breast
And ever for some weary soul
It breaths some tone of rest

Lucy E Larimer

(Lucy lived until 1900 and Brice did not die until 1906, he was then eighty-seven. History recalls Brice and Lucy as some of Elkhart County's pioneer settlers.)

Chapter Three

California - 1853 to 1909

Anonymous: We met the Light family on the California/Oregon Trail in 1853. My family was also heading west and like the Lights, were not part of an organized wagon train. Many people traveled solo, gathering together only at night for security. That was how we became acquainted with Emanuel, Elizabeth and their children.

We had other things in common with the Lights. Both families had not anticipated the extreme hardship of the trail; both families lost loved ones to cholera along the way and both families were forced to abandon many prized possessions along the trail, to lighten the load and help ensure survival. On the other hand, the Lights came to be a godsend for us as we were previously city-dwellers and not at all used to the toils of outdoor living, whilst they were already a rugged pioneer family. I am sure we would have fared much worse without their kind and wise counsel.

When not prevented by sheer, utter exhaustion, after the evening meal and after the provisions were stored we would sit around the campfire and tell stories, sing songs and recite favorite poems and verses we knew. The Lights had a wealth of poems which had been gathered in their commonplace book. They were happy to share them with us. Apparently it was begun years before in Ohio by Emanuel's first wife.

After the War of 1812 my father wrote this poem recalling a scene he had experienced at one of the engagements. I recited it one evening around the fire and Emanuel and Elizabeth insisted I enter it into their album. The album was so beautiful and the poems within so well written, I was honored to be included.

We traveled together until the trail split at Fort Hall, west of the Rocky Mountains. We proceeded on to Oregon while the Lights were bound for California.

The moon was softly beaming
Upon the terrible ground,
Its silver light was streaming
O'er the dying men around
A soldier weak and wounded
Who's form was filled with pain
Said smiling to his comrade
Shall I see my home again

♦ ♦ ♦ ♦

Jane L. Bently: I am one of two sisters of Elizabeth (Bently) Light, Emanuel's second wife. I was twenty-two when I wrote this poem.

We first *met* the Lights before we *became* the Lights, back in 1840 when Emanuel, Harriet and little David first showed up in Elkhart County, Indiana. My father befriended the Lights and it wasn't long before we loved them all. It was wild country back then, heavily wooded with settler's cabins spread out on their lands, usually a mile or more apart. There were fewer Indians by 1840. The Potawatomi had been forcibly evicted by the government and moved to the territories in 1838.

In 1852 little Frank was born to my sister and Emanuel. Shortly thereafter we packed our belongings and headed out for California during the Gold Rush. We crossed the Sierra Nevada Mountains and arrived before the snows in September of 1853.

I had the honor of writing the very first poem in Harriet's old album from California, even though it was yet another occurrence that was full of sorrow. Shortly after arriving in El-Dorado, my beloved brother-in-law David made up his mind to go off prospecting for gold. He was only fourteen years old at the time. Emanuel never would have let him go except he partnered up with a trusted family we had met on the trail. He did manage, later, to get a letter to us but I never saw him again. I wrote and entered this piece in the album the day after he left.

Cold Spring, Eldorad O, California, Sept 30, 53

To David Light

Can I forget the fond fond sigh
That breathed our last adieu
The tear that gemed thy lovely eye
Like dew on violets blue,

Though you and I no more may meet
Or be where we have been
Yet to dear rememberance sweet
Shall be our parting scene.

Jane L. Bently

♦ ♦ ♦ ♦

Jane L. Bently: My sister Elizabeth married Emanuel in 1847. My other sister, Lucy, also married in 1847 to Brice Larimer. Finally, in 1854 it was my turn. My betrothed, having had no luck as a prospector, had determined to quit that life and go to Oregon where he had relatives who encouraged us to join them. I was happy to have found a good man but I knew that leaving for Oregon meant a long if not permanent separation from my family. I was sad at that prospect. I wrote this poem in the album for them to remember me by and to let them know how much I would miss them.

It was ironic to me that very often getting married back then meant literally losing one family while acquiring another. It had happened to Harriet twenty years before. Now I must give up my beloved family to begin my own. Knowing that, my own wedding day was bittersweet. Such was the nature of being a settler. Significant change was inevitable. It was quite exciting to be there in the high Sierra Mountains, during the Gold Rush, yet life was insecure and uncertain. There was no law and order other than common courtesy, and that was often in short supply. The gold fever had attracted an unbelievable collection of people from everywhere and every walk of life, all trying their hand at prospecting and hoping to make their fortune. Why, it was positively International! While my new husband and I went north my family headed south to Tulare. They arrived there just in time for the Tule River Indian War of 1856. The Yokut Indians fought against the Tulare Mounted Riflemen.

The Bride's Farewell

California 1854

Farewell Brother tears are streaming
Down thy pale and tender cheek
I in gems and roses gleaming,
Scarce a sad fare-well can speak
Fare-well Mother now I leave thee
Hopes and fears my bosom swell
Trusting one who may deceive me
Fare-well Mother fare thee well

Fare-well Father thou art smiling,
Still, there's sadness on thy brow
Winning me from thats beguiling,
Fearless to which I go

Fare-well Father thou didst bless me
Ere thy name my life could tell

He may wound who can caress me
Father guardian fare - thee - well

Farewell Sister thou art training
Round me in affection deep
Wishing joy but mere divining,
Why a blessed bride should weep
Fare-well dear and gentle Brother
Thou art more dear than words can tell
Father Mother Sister Brother
All beloved ones fare ... thee ... well.

Jane L. Bently

♦ ♦ ♦ ♦

Martha Ann Light: I never knew Harriet. She died in 1843 and I wasn't born until 1855, in California. Nonetheless, I feel that I know her from seeing her through all her friend's eyes, through their poems to her. Father presented me with his first wife's Remembrance Album when I turned fifteen. He said that commonplace books were meant to be passed down from generation to generation and that it was now my turn to control the album and extend its life. I think this was my very first entry in the album.

Old Emanuel was thrilled to see the album come back to life. My friends and I filled the pages with new poems. Once we had exhausted the blank leaves, the album had been actively used for eight decades during which time somewhere around seventy people had turned its pages and left their hearts and souls within.

This is just a small portion of a wonderful poem by Christopher Pearce Cranch, entitled *Bird Language*. Both Father and I thought it worthy of entry into Harriet's album.

By the way, the poet, Mr. Cranch, was a Unitarian minister, author, poet, artist and member of the Transcendental Club. He lived in the Ohio Valley between 1837 and 1839 (another reason I thought it appropriate to be in Harriet's album). Mr. Cranch was a close friend of Emerson, Robert and Elizabeth Browning and James Russell Lowell. I loved it right away as my favorite subject is birdsong.

The Birds

One day in the bluest of summer weather
Sketching under a whispering oak
I heard five bobolinks laughing together
Over some ornithological joke
What the fun was I could not discover
Language of birds is a riddle on earth

♦ ♦ ♦ ♦

Anonymous: I suppose it serves me right. I did say after all, "Thou mayst these lines erase." I am not sure if Martha Ann actually did erase my poem or if it was just worn away over the years. One way or another most of it is barely legible now and parts are totally gone; that's what I get for writing in pencil. I do think the gist of the poem, however, is still discernable, and frankly, the ghostly image of the remnants of my poem are symbolic of the message contained therein.

I had lived a hard life and was not proud of some of the things I had done. Most folks steered clear of me but not Martha Ann. I lived on a little spread close to the Lights in Sonoma County and spent most of my time alone, except for my old dog and my horse. The old mutt hated everyone until Miss Martha Ann Light showed up on my doorstep one day. She befriended the both of us old curs and for that I was eternally grateful. She would stop by and visit us at least once a week.

Eventually she came to share her book of poetry, which I found immensely entertaining. I moved to Bodega Bay in 1880, but before I did I asked if I might make a contribution to her album. I hoped she might think of me upon occasion and I wanted to thank her for her kindness. I also wanted her to know that I saw great promise in her, she was such a bright, creative spirit.

Thou mayst these lines erase
If such thy wish should be
As pencileth friendship's trace
In trial's hour will flee
Life's joys are traced _____ _____
Its pleasures dust - they fly
Hope hath a magic wand
But tis illusive, I
Have felt, and known and lest
Sorrowed and wronged - full well
I know my joys shall be Lethe's rest
My hope - tis past - farewell!

But thou - the future's store
My wish with pleasure fills
With scenes of happiness and more
Support a _____ its ills
Among the shady groves
Thou treasure _____ and may dwell
No serpent's _____ - thy life be ____
Thy hope be heaven's - farewell!

♦ ♦ ♦ ♦

Martha Ann Light: From time to time I would leave a marker in the old album to remind me of an important occasion. The first marker, in 1870, was when the album was passed down to me. I was fifteen then, we lived in Tulare County. The second marked the year we left Tulare and moved north, the same year as the Modoc Indian War. By the end of 1872 the whole family ended up living in Santa Rosa, in the redwood-clad hills of Sonoma County, in northern California.

Martha Ann Light	May, 1870
Tuly River Tulare County	California

Tule River, January 9th 1872	Martha A. Light

♦ ♦ ♦ ♦

Anonymous: I transcribed this little ditty into Martha Light's old album when we both lived in Tulare County, however, they had plans to move soon. We was both seventeen years old at the time and had been good friends who spent many happy hours exploring the countryside around our homes. I hoped she would remember me. I knew I would remember her.

She and her folks helped me learn to read and write with the aid of their old poetry album. I gained an appreciation for verse in those days. These words were written by John B. Adams, in 1849, as sheet music; the music was by George O. Farmer.

Ulysses S. Grant was still President then. He was a much better General than he was a President, in my opinion. General George Cook had begun his campaign against the Apaches earlier this year, in the Arizona Territory. The Battle of the Little Big Horn would not happen for another four years. This old verse sounds best when recited with a burly Irish accent.

Remembered

'Tis sweet to be remembered
In the turmoils of this life,
While toiling up its pathways,
While mingling in its strife;
While wandering o'er earths borders
Or sailing on the sea,

'Tis sweet to be remembered,
Where ever we may be.

March (16th 1872)

♦ ♦ ♦ ♦

Anonymous: It was indeed my pleasure to have the Light family attend my little church in Santa Rosa, California. It was in 1875 as I recall. Miss Martha Ann asked me if I would copy a portion of one of my sermons into the family commonplace book. She felt it a worthy apothegm and I was touched to be included in the family heirloom album.

I came to California from Pennsylvania back in the 1850's, to spread the Word and see these lands, known then by many as El-Dorado. I never looked back. Many of the poets in the Light poetry album say that one should not put too much stock in earthly pleasures. Of course I agree in theory, but would have to surmise...none of them lived in California! The mild agreeable climate and lovely landscapes are hard to resist, as far as earthly pleasures go.

Let me save you a trip to the dictionary. A 'clepsydra' is an ancient complicated water clock. Can you see how the West affected my speech? I never would have used a phrase like "and whip us with our own policy" back east.

"Never deceive any one! Even to their own good, as thou may'st think; for thou knowest not what little circumstance may intervene, unknown to thee, and, scattering all the good designs to the wind, nay leave the deceit alone, to act deep and mischievously

A grain of sand in the tubes of a clepsydra will derange all its functions, and throw its manifold and complicated movements wrong. How much more likely, then, that some little unforeseen accident in the intricate workings of this great earthly machine

should prove our best calculations false, and whip us with our own policy! Oh never, never deceive!
Deceit in itself is evil, and intention can never make it good."

♦ ♦ ♦ ♦

F.B.S.: I was crazy about Martha Light. She was, bar none, the prettiest gal on the Tuly River in 1872. I wrote this when her family was moving north, to Santa Rosa, in Sonoma County. At one time I considered myself a fair candidate for Martha's affection. Alas, it was not to be. I bid her farewell and hoped she might think of me from time to time. I knew I would never forget her, nor the old book of poetry she loved so much.

Oct 12th 1872

When other life and other hearts
Their tale of love shall tell,
In language whose excess imparts,
The power they feel so well.
There may perhaps in such a scene,
Some recolection be,
Of days that have as happy been
And you'll remember me.

When coldness or deceit - shall stile
The beauty now thy prize,
And deem it but a faded light
Which beams with in your eyes,
When hollow hearts shall wear a mask
Twill break your own to see,
In such a moment I but ask,
That you'll remember me.

F.B.S.

♦ ♦ ♦ ♦

Anonymous: After so many poems with either mournful or fatalistic themes Martha Ann wanted something a little more cheery, as a contrast. She asked me to enter this rhyme, which I wrote, into her album. I courted Martha Ann for awhile but as you can see from the fact that my name has been scraped away, we had a falling out.

Pleasanter than All

Robins in the tree tops
Blossoms in the grass
Green things are growing
Every where you pass
Sudden little breeze
Showers of lith silver dew
Black bough and branch tiny
Budding out anew
Pine trees and willow trees
Fringed elm and larch
Don't you think that May time
Is pleasanter than March?

(*Name has been scraped away*)

♦ ♦ ♦ ♦

Anonymous: After Abraham Lincoln had freed us, our family came out here to California and we got our own land. We came to be neighbors with the Light family. They were all so kind to us and treated us as equals. That was rare indeed. Mrs. Elizabeth insisted I come to their house for home-schooling with her children. She taught me to read and write. We often read the poems in the old album, which I loved. I memorized quite a few. Martha and I were pretty much the same age and became fast friends. I copied this poem into the album back in the 1870's, when they left Tulare and moved up north. We wrote letters to each other for years after.

Accept this fom your friend

Accept this gift this little gift
A token of my love for thee
Whenever towards it thou shalt lift
Thine eyes - oh then remember me.

Remember that there still is one
Who till the sun shall cease to shine
Will love - till from earth she's gone
Her latest prayer shall ere be thine.

And mayst thou never want a friend
Since thou hast been so kind to me
And Oh, may Heaven each moment bring
Its soothing sweetest aid to thee

Oh may the smiles of bounteous Heaven
For ever guide the(*e*) here below
May all delight, all joys be given
To thee, who dost dese(*r*)ve no more.

♦ ♦ ♦ ♦

Martha Ann Light: I wish I had dated my poems. As I recall, I wrote this poem when U.S. Grant was President, in 1871. The outlaws Jesse and Frank James were very active then –not where we lived, of course! We were in Tulare County, California at the time. It was then a great expanse of fertile farmland between the Pacific Ocean to the west and the Sierra Nevada Mountains to the east. Tulare is an Indian word meaning 'tall rushes' and the grass was often so high that it would come up to a horse's shoulders. Tule Elk were a common sight in those days. I loved to sit outdoors and watch the clouds passing overhead. It was on one of these occasions when I was inspired to write this poem.

The Cloud

A white white cloudlet up in the sky,
Borne on the winds, and of the waves am I.
And soft I float thru the tremulous blue,
When the shining stars of heaven peep through.
I cover them often from mortal sight,
And hold in my bosom their silvery light
And the moon enfolds me with soft embrace,
And smiles upon me with silvery face.
The sun climbing high in the rosy morn,
My whiteness tint with color of dawn
And around me shield through the long long day
The glory and light of his shining ray!
And the lark springs forth in the morning sweet,
And sings me songs from the dawning meet.
While he plunges deep in my snowy maze
The stains of earth from his pinions to lave.
When the sun sinks deep in the far far west
O'er a purple billow with golden crest
And stains with his glory the mountain dim
And lingers with crimson on my curling rim
And the twilight dies while the night birds sing
And darkness sweeps downward on noiseless wing
Then again I hold in my bosom white
The deep shining stars with their silvery light.

M.A.L.

♦ ♦ ♦ ♦

Anonymous: My poem was for Miss Martha Light. Lord, she was charming! And such a kind nature. She always brought out the best in whomever she was with.

I'll Always Think of Thee

The blossoms fade the flowers blow
The stream runs to the sea.
But time may come and time may go
I'll always think of thee,

Inconstant is the word for all
Change is and is to be
But thrones may rise and thrones may fall
I'll always think of thee

♦ ♦ ♦ ♦

Martha Ann Light: I had heard Mr. Stephen Foster's song long before I wrote it down in the album. It was written four years before I was born, in 1851. I understand it was the most popular song ever published at the time and was known the world over. If it hadn't been for Luther I would have never considered writing a song in my father's first wife's album. There were no other songs in the album; I thought perhaps she would not have approved. That was in 1870, two years before the Modoc Indian War up in northern California.

We met Mr. Luther Brown, around 1863, in Tulare County. I was only eight at the time and remember because of the war. Abraham Lincoln was then the President. Luther was a runaway slave from the Deep South. Though he did not like to speak of those days I do know that he had no family so he was able to slip away from his master and proceeded to get as far away as he could. No one was sure who would win the war at that point. And so he began his journey west. He walked the entire way.

When he ended up in California, my father gave him a job and roof over his head. Luther could not read or write but had a fine singing voice. You could hear him singing half a mile away. He always sang no matter what he was doing, chopping wood, working with us in the garden or just sitting on the porch.

He was almost fifty when I was old enough to start writing my own poetry. Luther, by that point was a part of the family. Everyone in the family wrote at least one entry in the album. I thought Luther should also. After getting Father's permission I asked Luther to sing a song which I would write down and he could make his mark. This is what he selected. He would not admit it but I suspect he wrote part of the middle verses. I have checked and it does not appear to be a part of Mr. Foster's original song.

The Old Folks at Home

A way down upon the Swanee River
Far far away
Theres where my heart is turning ever
Thers where the old folks stay

All up and down the whole creation
Sadly I roam
Still longing for the old plantation
And for the old folks at home

All the world seems sad and dreary
Every where I roam
Oh! Brothers how my heart grows weary
Far from the old folks at home

All around the little farm I wandered
When I was young
There many pleasant days I've squandered
Many songs I've sung

When I was playing with my brother
Happy was I
Oh, take me to my kind old mother
There let me live and die

When I was in the field a hoeing
Near the set of sun
Glad to hear the horn a blowin
To tell that the work was done

Then the darkeys frolick sweetly
Banjo in tune
Dine and Fillie dressed so neetly
Danced by the big round moon

One little hut among the bushes
One whoom I do love
Still fondly to my memory rushes
No mater where I rove

When will I hear the bees a humming
All among the comb
When will I hear the banjo tuning
Down in my good old home

All the world seems sad and dreary
Every where I roam
Oh! Brothers how my heart grows weary
Far from the old folks at home

L.B.x.

♦ ♦ ♦ ♦

Lucien Light: I am the final child born to my parents, Emanuel and Elizabeth Light. I was born in 1868 when my mother was forty-seven years old and I have the unique distinction of having written what must be characterized as the sole failure in Harriet's album. Of course she was then long in the grave. It was my sister Martha's album when I wrote my little failure. Martha warned me to prepare my poem as a draft and then to make my entry into the album, transcribing from my draft, so I would avoid errors in the album. I didn't listen, made an irreparable mistake and gave it up.

Martha was very angry with me and said it was disrespectful to all the other poets in the album who were so careful with their entries.

In early spring when I was young
I used to skip about
In mery glee but when
Hot summer came i got
So mad i did not what to do

♦ ♦ ♦ ♦

Martha Ann Light: When I wrote this, all I had ever known was a two-room cabin for a home. My father told us about Harriet's home in Ohio. It was two stories of heavy timber construction with many rooms. They had servants, for gosh sakes. I never saw anything like that until we moved to Sonoma County. We went right through San Francisco on our way. It was the first 'city' I had ever been to. We saw houses there that I imagined were like Harriet's house. I wish I had known her.

This poem is based on a true story. I had a little sparrow which I nursed back to health after it broke its wing. He tamed down during that time and afterwards was a pet, seemingly happy to stay with us. Birdie, as I called him, followed me around outdoors. He would spend each night on a perch I gave him, next to my bed. We lost him on a winter's night when he went out in a howling wind and was blown away, never to return.

Birdie

One beautiful day in the winter
Two birds came near our door
We opened, and bade them a welcome
To our heart, to our home, evermore

I chose the blue eyes, for my darling
I nestled him close to my heart
I wrapped love's cloak round my darling
And whispered oh never depart

One cold, bitter night in the winter
The storm came, the rain fell so fast
I opened the door and my birdie
Went out in the cold wintry blast

Come back to my hearthstone my birdie
And the fire will burn as of yore
The cricket will sing in the corner
And pet we'll rejoice ever more

♦ ♦ ♦ ♦

Eugene Light: You may have noticed, while reading the various love poems in my mother's album, that young love was an outdoor sport back in the 1800's. Our small settler's cabins afforded no privacy whatsoever and so love tended to bloom outdoors, where young people could be alone.

I proposed to my wife, Nannie E. Robinson, at Green Valley Falls. It is a beautiful little spot on Green Valley Creek, outside of Sebastopol, California. Happily for me she said yes and we were married November 2, 1870. I wrote this poem shortly thereafter but did not enter it into mother's album until a few years later, after the rest of my family had moved up here from Southern California.

Martha, my half-sister, ruled the Remembrance Album back in those days and insisted that every member of the family enter at least one poem. This was my one and only entry.

Green Valley Falls

Can fairy lands be like to thee,
Green Valley Falls?
Thou seemst to me e'en heavenly,
For here I heard my destiny

Beside thy rippling shady stream
Green Valley Falls;
I felt the sweets of Love's fair dream
A guiding star thou e'er dids't seem,

For she sat smiling by my side
Green Valley Falls;
And said if wealth or woe betide
I'll be thy own -thy faithful bride.

♦ ♦ ♦ ♦

Martha Ann Light: This old saying, from the Revolution days, I copied from a newspaper. It is a time honored truth and thus was appropriate for Harriet's album. Not only that, I always thought of Harriet as a woman of action and not just speech, to do what she did. I grew up the child of a settler and never knew anything different. Harriet, on the other hand, left everything of her rich life behind to follow her heart and her dream, and live like us, as poor farmers in the Far West.

I suppose it is odd that the whole family, even my mother, loved Harriet. Both mother and father would always say, "what would Harriet have done?" as if she were the example for how we should behave. I guess she was.

Speech without action is a moral dearth
And to advance the world is little worth
Let us think much say little and much
Do, if to ourselves and god we will be true.

♦ ♦ ♦ ♦

Anonymous: Martha Light was a good, dear friend. She and I spent many hours reading the poetry in her family's old album. We liked to muse on the circumstances which brought about its creation and how beautiful Harriet Light must have been. Martha's pa told stories, from the Ohio days, about Harriet; stories of how Harriet had dressed in the latest fashions, with all the frills. Harriet's mother employed only the finest dress makers. Martha Ann and I had only seen pretty dresses like that in newspapers and magazines; all of our clothes were homemade from simple gingham.

Martha invited me to write a poem in the album but unlike her I was not much of a writer. We were both lovers of all forms of nature. Martha loved birds and birdsong and I loved flowers so I wrote two of my favorite verses. The first is from the New Testament, Matthew 6:28 and the second verse is from James Gates Percival's "The Language of Flowers." Mr. Percival was a popular contemporary poet when I wrote this entry.

Consider the lillies of the field;
They toil not neither do they spin;
Yet Soloman in all his glory was
Not arrayed like one of these

In eastern lands they talk in flowers
And tell in a garland their loves and cares
Each blossom that blooms in our garden love
On its leaves a mystic language bears;

♦ ♦ ♦ ♦

Martha Ann Light: I liked Mr. Holmes's poem; it is the only patriotic piece in the album. My family is very patriotic, so I thought this poem appropriate for the family's Remembrance

Album. Mr. Holmes wrote this in 1861. President Lincoln had just been elected and the War Between the States was just beginning. Of course I was only a child in 1861, six years old. I didn't transcribe it into the album until the late 1870s when we lived in Sonoma County, California. There are two verses missing. The following page was already used so I had to make do with one page and was unable to fit the entire poem onto it. I had to do some editing.

The Flower of Liberty

"What flower is this that greets the morn
Its hues from heaven so freshly born?
With burning stars and flaming band
It kindles all the sunset land;
Oh tell us what its name may be!
Is this the flower of Liberty?
It is the banner of the free
The starry flower of Liberty?

In savage nature's far abode
It's tender seeds our father's sowed
The storm winds racked its swelling bud
It's opening leaves were streaked with blood
Till, lo! Earth's tyrants shrank to see
The full blown flower of Liberty
Then hail the banner of the free
The starry flower of Liberty
Thy sacred leaves fair freedom's power
Shall ever float on dome and tower
To all their heavenly colors true
In blacking frost or crimson dew
And God loves us as we love thee
Thrice holy flower of Liberty
Then hail the banner of the free
The starry flower of Liberty!"

♦ ♦ ♦ ♦

Anonymous: Shoot, I couldn't believe Martha Ann wanted me to write something in her shrine. That's what she called that poem book she was never without. We met Martha here in Santa Rosa back in 1875. She was as fine as a spring day, always had a smile or good word for everyone.

My family's farm was next to the Light place on the outskirts of town. Martha Ann would stop by to visit and sometimes she'd read us poems. Some she wrote, others were from folks she never even knew but had written in that same book. I didn't really understand but they were some mighty fine poems. My wife, Caroline, would fix Miss Martha some lemonade and she and the youngsters and I would sit on the porch and listen to her verses.

One day she asked me if I knew any poetry. I had written a poem, back when I was of courting age and was trying to steal the heart of my true love. Martha Ann said she thought it was just right and asked me to write it in her old book. I can't write real fancy like the other folks in the book and made something of a mess. All the same Miss Martha said it was her new favorite and seemed pleased.

To
Caroline of Dricreek

Its of a fare young damsel,
A story - I will tell she was a
Farmer's daughter dear
on Dricreek she did dwell
Her hare was like the ravens wing
Her eyes like stars did shine
And red as roseys was the cheeks
Of sweet Caroline

♦ ♦ ♦ ♦

Martha Ann Light: I was married in 1882 in Santa Rosa, California. Chester A. Arthur was the President then and the shootout between the Earps and Clantons at the OK Corral occurred that year. My husband was a fine man and we had many happy years together. We lived on a small farm near my older brother Eugene's place. It was also close to father and mother's farm. We were all in a lovely valley between the green hills. Coast oaks, and giant redwoods ruled in most places, interspersed with clearings for farms and homes. With the fine mild weather of California, we never lacked for food. We also had orchards of apple trees. Our county was becoming known as a producer of fine apples. My favorites are the Gravenstein apples, a species native to Denmark but adopted by folks in Sonoma County as their own.

Life was good for us then. California truly was the land of milk and honey. You could practically drop a seed on the ground and it would grow. It rained in the winter but never got really cold. Father used to tell us of how cold, wet and miserable winters had been back in Indiana and Ohio. I could not imagine it, having lived my entire life in the West. I had seen snow on the distant mountains, but at that time had never visited them.

I spent a lot of time working on my poetry, in the evenings, after chores and supper. This was written after two years of marriage. I think we were as passionate then as father and Harriet had been so long ago.

Father and mother do love each other very much but have never been all that passionate, not like it was with Harriet. My parents are the first to admit that they did not marry for love. Both of mother's parents died in Indiana in the 1840s, leaving just the three sisters. In those tough days in Indiana neither Emanuel nor the Bently girls could run a farm by themselves. As good friends with respect for each other, Mother and Father understood that fact and so they were married back in 1847. Love came with time for my parents. I asked my mother once if she wasn't even a little jealous of Harriet and how we all knew so much about 'the first wife.' The fact that I had Harriet's commonplace book by itself meant that Harriet was still very much a part of our family. Mother laughed and said no, she wasn't jealous. She felt the same way about Harriet. They had been close friends.

To My Husband
Since I Knew Thee!

The spring is coming with her flowers
To bid the heaven and earth be gay;
To breathe a "pledge of happier hours,
And chase all gloomier thoughts away."
The young birds hear her welcome voice
And 'mid the budding trees rejoice
I join them in their songs of gladness
And feel the happiness I see
Yet I have known no thought of sadness
Since I knew thee!

Mine are the prouder hopes of life,
The hopes that cannot dread decay
To meet and grapple on the way
The thoughts that thrill, the joys that bless
That language neve(*r*) can express -
All all are mine my bosom's treasure.
Hopes, joys, and thoughts the happy three
My life has been a life of pleasure,
Since I knew thee!

♦ ♦ ♦ ♦

Martha Ann Light: For clarity, all the poems are ordered more or less chronologically in this manuscript, but in the old album this short, sweet poem can be found towards the front of the album, next to a poem by Mary Hildreth. They were written some forty years apart.

Lovely songsters of the air
Sound your note of gladness
Drive away our thoughts of care
Sing away our sadness

♦ ♦ ♦ ♦

Anonymous: Martha Light and I grew up together in Tulare County, California. After chores we could usually be found riding horses, swimming in the river or just lying around trying to imitate birdsong. Martha was a very good whistler and could imitate many birds.

Throughout the nineteenth century, writing and reciting poetry was a popular pastime. Both Martha and I felt we were decent poets and we were always sharing our poems with each other. When in the 1870's, the Lights decided to move up to Sonoma County, I wrote this poem for Martha to remember me by. Inasmuch as her favorite poetic subject was birdsong, I hoped she would like this poem and read it often when she might think of our happy years together.

The Lovely Whippoorwill

The sun hath declined beneath the blue wave
The dew drops of evening the wild flowers leave
The gentle queen of night beams on yonder ripling rill
While I listen to the notes of the lovely Whippoorwill

No more shall the poet be proud of her lay
Apollo must yield to the music of the spray
Not the taber on the plain or the music on the rill
Can equal the notes of the lovely Whippoorwill

The robin may sing her sweet sonnet of love
And, the philomel warbler his notes in the grove
Their soft and gentle lay may my soul with rapture fill
But they cannot be compared to the lovely Whippoorwill

On life('s) rugged paths a few roses we find
Their hope seems elusive and fate seems sinking
Should fortune on me frown I would smile upon her still
While pleasure(*d*) in the notes of the lovely Whippoorwill

♦ ♦ ♦ ♦

Martha Ann Light: I was quite the self-made ornithologist and could whistle many bird songs. Birds are nature's orchestra, providing a daily symphony, free to all. You have only to listen. I was quite proud of this poem as I think I achieved my goal. I was trying to write a poem which would sound like, or be a metaphor for, a real bird symphony. By the way, "chewink" is another name for a towhee.

Bird Songs

When the rosy light of day
O'er the hillside flushes
Then begins the reverellay
Of the happy thrushes

Soon as misty shades of night
From the valleys clear up
Robin sings with all his might
Cheer up; cheer up; cheer up;

Chris-chris cradle silver song,
Rings among the ledge
Chipping sparrow chip along,
All the dreary hedges,

The bee by the tinkling rills
Sings with wrens and swallows
Merry bobolincoln trills
O'er the grassy hollows
Mellow lay so clear and rare
Sweet chewink is ringing
From his castle in the air.

♦ ♦ ♦ ♦

Martha Ann Light: Winter was such a hard season for the settler families in northern Indiana. The temperature was too often well below zero with snow falling in blizzards. We kids used to listen to our father's stories about those days. Having been born later and raised in California, where winters are very mild, I had never experienced a really hard winter. It was my father's stories mainly that inspired this poem. All the good things in life disappeared in those Indiana winters. Color was replaced by the unyielding white of snow and ice or the empty black of night. All the birds and their songs went away to leave only silence. The flowers and plants shriveled, beauty indeed did perish. The loss of these living things for the endless void of winter was literally painful to those settler families, according to my father.

To the Humming Bird

Oh, tell me little humming bird
O'er, the garden flying
Are all the zephyrs gone away
Are all the flowers dying
The lillies and the golden buds
Golden flowers we cherish
Oh must they wither and depart
Must their beauty perish

And shall we by the river roam
Vainly seeking for them
When they are slumbering with the rest
That have gone before them
We would we saw the lillies gleam
Where the waters shinning
Where lowly lean the willow boughs
Vines round them twining

We would we saw the sunflower rise,
Golden o'er the meadow
And gaze upon the days red eye
Laughing at the shadow!

We would we heard the wildbirds sing
Mong their leafy bowers
But they have vanished ere the rest
Gone before the flowers,

Yes all are passing; passing; all
Things of earth are fading
The beautiful the bright the fair
Time is ever shading
And we who linger to the last
Watch the rest departing
We know how sad it is to lose
Know it by the smarting

♦ ♦ ♦ ♦

M.T.L.: Chasing the ambitions of this earthly life should not take precedence over taking the time to reflect on and give thanks for the best things in life. We should not spend so much time admiring ourselves for our cleverness or seeking wealth. What is really important in life is taking the time to appreciate friends and family. We should strive to do good works for others and not just for ourselves. Harriet was the “trembling spirit” winging her flight into the unknown, not for riches or fame, but to be with the man she loved and to explore the yet unknown West. To do that she had to separate herself from people who insisted she become someone she was not. Harriet cared less for wealth than she did for people and adventure. She preferred to spend time with her friends discovering heaven on earth. What made her rich was sharing some new joy with a friend, the song of a bird or finding a bright field of wild flowers. These were the things which brought Harriet Pruden happiness. She may not have lived a long life but in that short time there were many ‘well spent hours.’

The Well Spent Hour

Lighter than air, hope's summer vision fly,
If but a fleeting cloud obscure the sky,
If but a beam of sober reason play
Lo! Fancy's fairy frostwork melts away -
But can the wiles of art, the grasp of power
Snatch the rich relics of the well spent hour
These, when the trembling spirit wings her flight
Pour round her path a stream of living light
And gild those pure and perfect realms of rest
Where virtue triumphs and her sons are blest

Transcribed by your friend M.T.L.

♦ ♦ ♦ ♦

The End

Epilogue

By 1890 records indicate only Emanuel, Eugene and his wife Nannie were still living in northern California. What became of Martha Ann and the other Lights is unknown to this author. Santa Rosa is only a short distance from San Francisco so perhaps they rode out the big earthquake of 1906 in Eugene's house on Slater Street. Santa Rosa was virtually destroyed but the house is still standing and occupied to this day.

After its active life was over, the old album must have survived, cherished, for years in the Light family. Somehow it slipped away from them and found its way to me as if to say:

> *Now one hundred and seventy-five years after I was begun everyone is gone, except inside me. I have tried my best to protect them –Harriet, her friends and family. It was my destiny to accompany them, also my honor. Like an ancient tree, I have seen so much. I have survived all these years to keep my unspoken pledge to Harriet. My duty, and now yours, is to make sure all of them are remembered.*

Postscript

R.C. (Rebecca) Pruden: Harriet and I were opposites. She was the rebel and I the conformist to the Cult of Domesticity. She wanted adventure and I wanted a long, secure, cultured life. In 1836 Harriet eloped and headed west. That same year I married Soloman Clippenger and stayed in the East.

In retrospect I wish I had gone with Harriet and Emanuel. Perhaps I would have seen and experienced more of the world. But instead I died, along with my baby in childbirth, nine months after my wedding. I was twenty-eight.

A final note on my album, known as, *Rebecca's Red Book*. After my death it was passed on to my brother Charles' wife, Caroline. Eventually they also went west and found themselves in Missouri at the beginning of the war between the states. Along with my album, one of Caroline's letters to her daughter Achsa has survived. Mr. Pate and I both thought it appropriate to include that letter in this work as it so aptly describes how tenuous life was in the West. This letter was written over twenty years after Harriet had made her way into the wilderness. Not to make light of Caroline's difficult circumstance, but in comparison, what Harriet had to endure would make Caroline's life seem a tea party.

Albany, January 6th, 1862
My Deare Achsa,

Youre kind letter of Nov 25th came to hand
and I have delayed writing longuer than usual upon the
reason I have been chilling every third day and some
times shaking at night and you may think I did not
feel like doing anything but mope around I have
Got better now and intend to answer your letter
Altorf has got his legs cured and has better health than
at any time sinse we came to Missouri The rest are all
well John gets all the work he can do but cannot get
but little money every thing is plenty but clothing and

it is hard to get any thing to weare the merchants will not bring on goods the boys had to go to St. Lo to get salt they took a load of hickory-nuts and got some things that we could not do without domestic is 20 cts per yard coffy 25 cts a lb calico 15 cts per yard and salt one dollar per bushel and every thing else in proportion I would like to know how you spent youre christmas we spent oures at home we had no companey but ourselves we war all to gather this christmas we have a good warme house one rome is sealed and one plastered a good fireplase and plenty of wood we have plenty to live on and can get all the apples we want where John is at work John gets alongue very well they think he does every thing just right
Frank is in his glory he has hogs and sheep and chickens and turkeys to feed we have 10 lambs and they require some care this colde weather but we have a good barne oure horses do not stand shivering in the colde and snow like they did last winter I can tell you thare has a change come over us for the better we had no difficulty where we lived they had a son in law come to se them from Iowa and he thought he would stay and farme the plase if we arve willing and we happened on the plase it was a meare accident Judge Howels boys left home and went in the Southern army and he moved to town and was anxious to have us go in the house as soon as they left one of his boys have got home and the other they heare nothing of I suppose you heare great accounts of this part of the state there is now in Albany about 600 armed men union of corse and they are playing the mischief with all rebels taking prisinors every day they and taking graine and every thing they can get from the rebbels they do not allow man woman or child to call Jef Davis name in the streets nor to call them Abolition.
When this trouble will end is hard to tell we

heare so many reports but get no papers   I have
not been able to get the message and I would
like to see it so well tell Call to send me
a paper if he can
Now Achsa how longue we will stay heare I do not
know but I expect we will stay on this farme
until we leave the state   if the war continues
and Missouri has to be kept in the union by forse
it will be the best for us to leave as soon as
we can and if they get quiet and all setteled
we may by a farme heare but when I think
of you being away so far   I feel like I could not
endure the thought of being heare but I must do
what is the best for all   The boys have a better
prospect for makein property now than they have
sinse we came west and if I can have my health
I will help them all I can   Emma has got so
she can do the moste of the work when I am
not able!
An other day has gone and I have not got to send
my letter to town and I will sribble some more   I hope
you will soon be in a house to youre self   Spring will
soon be heare and you must be patient as you can
Aunt Harriet has been out to see me onse and
Eliza Jane stayed with me a week   they are nearly
all a chilling and one of the girls stays with
Caroline White   she has been a cripple for a bout
a yeare and I think it is doubtful if ever she gets well
we get no news from Kansas nor I have not heard
from Oscar for a long time. There is a fine snow on the
ground and I would like to have a sleigh-ride but
the boys have no time for sport
I have not been from home sinse we came out
heare and do not expec to go soon   it is not
safe for people to go from home heare for they
do not know whether they will have a hoouse when they
come back   there has been several houses burned
lately while the folks ware absent.
There is no Schools in the country any more

no public money it was all taken to support the
war I try two have the boys at there book all I
can and Emma is very good to read she has
no company nor nothing to take her attention from her
book. Now Achsa I must close my letter I want
you to write often as you can if you knew how glad I am to
heare from you you would write Emma has some wild
columbine seed to send you in the spring they are the richest
wild flower I ever saw I wish I could be with you to
help you make garden in the spring I am glad
you got some strawberrys and you must get some
gooseberryes there is plenty of wild snowberryes hear

I never saw as many as I did last summer
now I have got my sheet nearly full and I must
say good by to you all
Caroline Pruden
write soon to not forget youre poore
olde mother

Conclusion

One of the many interesting aspects of Harriet's old album is that it was almost continually on the far western edge of our country. As the border to the States moved further and further west, so did the album and it's owners. It and they were firsthand witnesses to almost the entire century of Westward Expansion, from a participant's point of view.

Often when some wonderful old object is found we say, "If only it could talk, what a story it could tell!" Harriet's album can and does speak for itself. Imagine reading only the poems, as I did. It was clear from the start there was a story behind them. The album is a Narrative Poetry Anthology, a term I coined, which is defined as "a collection of poems by multiple authors which chronicle the same story, in real time, as the story unfolds or progresses." As far as I know, it is the only one of its kind.

Poetry is such an intimate and revealing art form that we get to see much about Harriet and about the authors. Through their own words we sense their hopes, their fears, their attitudes about life, death, love, beauty, religion and friendship. Through their words we are immersed in the Zeitgeist of their time. We get a good sense of who (at least some of) the early settler's were, those who came behind the pioneers and claimed and settled the new lands. We also meet the people who do not want Harriet to venture west. They tell us why, in their own words and verses.

The opening chapter is as much Athens, Ohio's story as it is Harriet's. It was the right time, in the right place, with the right people, that led to Harriet's drive to go west and thus to the album's creation. Harriet's parents and their friends had, years before, been pioneer settlers themselves. Harriet had the same resolve. One comes quickly to understand, through the poetry, that Harriet was determined to go, even if she was considered naive and/or innocent.

Harriet is a first generation American, if you start counting after the *second* American Revolution (The War of 1812). After that war, America is a more mature country, more confident and free from European Imperialism. The continent was ripe for the taking. The eyes of America slowly but earnestly turned west ... the time was right.

The right people were in Athens. It was a college town, the University attracted people who loved literature. They were well-educated people who took advantage of the library of Ohio University. They were exposed to the latest popular poetry via the library and newspapers. It was their literary expertise that set the high standard of the album, a standard which would be adhered to for decades, even after Harriet's death. The album would not exist if it had not been for the creative souls of Athens, Ohio.

The album readily gives up certain tantalizing clues. The dated poems reveal its age. The places noted tell, in broad strokes, where it has been. We find out quickly from the messages in the early poems that an adored young woman is leaving home; seemingly forever and into harm's way. We also see that it is a wonderfully compiled album. From the finely embroidered bouquet on the cover to the well-composed and penned poems within, this was a lot of work for a lot of people, which tells us how much Harriet meant to them. Those are the obvious clues.

Other pieces of the story were more difficult to come by. The conclusion that Harriet and Emanuel eloped is a best guess based on the information at hand. First, while no one actually mentions a boyfriend by name, it was clear there was a man involved. Single, well-to-do young ladies just didn't leave home in those days, they *had* to be somehow chaperoned or married. Second, Harriet may well have been engaged as early as 1831 but no one from Athens, except for A.G. Brown, even mentions the possibility of marriage. If your friends and family are happy about your betrothal wouldn't they say so? Of course they would, but we find not a single congratulation, instead we find people extremely worried for Harriet's future.

Did the young couple really elope? There are important clues of omission. Emanuel's name was never once mentioned or written in the album in the Athens period, and as noted above, marriage was alluded to only once or twice in an off-handed way, no doubt because it was generally considered an unwelcome occurrence. Another important indication is that Harriet and Emanuel were married in Logan in 1837. With all the friends that Harriet clearly had, if the wedding had been welcome at home they would have married in Athens, likely years before. After all, the album was begun in 1831. Harriet and Emanuel apparently tried for six years to be accepted as a couple and then we find them being married well away from Athens.

The young couple very likely eloped, but other scenario's are possible. The historical record shows that Silas and Mary, Harriet's parents, also left Athens in 1837. They also moved to Logan, in Hocking County. The financial crash of 1837 certainly played a role in their move but the historical record shows that in addition to a house in Logan they owned a 40 acre tract nearby. This indicates that Silas was not left penniless by the financial climate; but it also might suggest that the young couple simply waited until family financial woes made it the right time for them to break away and follow their original plan. The ultimate outcome in any scenario is that Harriet and Emanuel leave for Indiana. There are no other records yet found which can verify these assertions. The album tells it's own story but the details are lost.

The important job of determining which poems were original and which copied into the album from another source was taken on by Jeanette Berard, Research Librarian, of the Thousand Oaks Library System. These are her findings. Twenty-five percent of the poems were transcribed into the old album from verified, published sources, usually from well known and popular authors of the time. The most likely source of the published version was a book, newspaper or magazine in the Athens period; thereafter, most likely source was from newspapers. Of the balance it is likely that another twenty-five percent is transcribed from elsewhere, but that source did not survive long enough or was simply lost before being "indexed" anywhere. That leaves roughly fifty percent of these verses to be classified as original "folk-poems."

Whether original or not most of the poems seem to mirror or reflect contemporary thought of the time. The album gives, in addition to everything else, an idea of what was popular in Harriet's day and throughout the 1800's.

Eugene, Harriet's youngest, marries Nannie Robinson in Santa Rosa, California, November 2, 1870. The 1880 census shows the whole remaining Light clan had also moved north from Tulare County to Santa Rosa (in Sonoma County) and includes: Emanuel (64), Elizabeth (59), Frank (27), Martha (25) and Lucien (18). They all worked the family farm together in the Lewis district.

The amazing adventure of Harriet's album does not end until 1909, eighty years after the journey began. Ironically, the most recent period in the album has the least amount of information available on the people in it. It remains unknown what became of the Light family after 1890. The exception is Eugene, who is buried in Rural Cemetery in Santa Rosa, California. He died "a well-respected man" on July 25, 1908 at sixty-eight years of age. There is also a bit more about Eugene's wife, Nannie. The final entry in the album is a journalistic entry in regards to a luncheon given in honor of Nannie. It was given by a Mrs. Kate Blow, in Los Angeles in 1909, one year after Eugene's death.

Emanuel, unlike Harriet, lived a long life and is listed in the Sonoma County 1890 census at seventy-five years of age. Only he and Eugene are listed. The 1890 census was destroyed by fire and has been only partially reconstructed.

There may well be hundreds, if not thousands, of descendants of the contributors to Harriet's album, alive today. If you are one of these people please contact the author and tell him who you are, and who you descend from. If you have any more information on this old, wonderful story, please share it. Thank you.

Photographs

"May Cloudless beams of grace and truth
Adorn my daughters opening youth;
Long happy in her native home,
Among its fragrant groves to roam,
May choisest blessings her attend.
In Parents Brothers Sisters friends;
May no rude wish assail her breast
to love this world by all confest
Is only given us to prepare
For one eternal, bright and fair
This world shall then no force retain
Its syren voice shall charm in vain
Religions aid true peace will bring,
Her voice with joy shall praises sing
To him whose streames of mercy flow
To cheer the heart over charged with woe
And whilst retirements sweets we prove
Forever praise redeeming love,,

Mary Pruden

Mary Pruden's poem to her daughter, Harriet, page 6

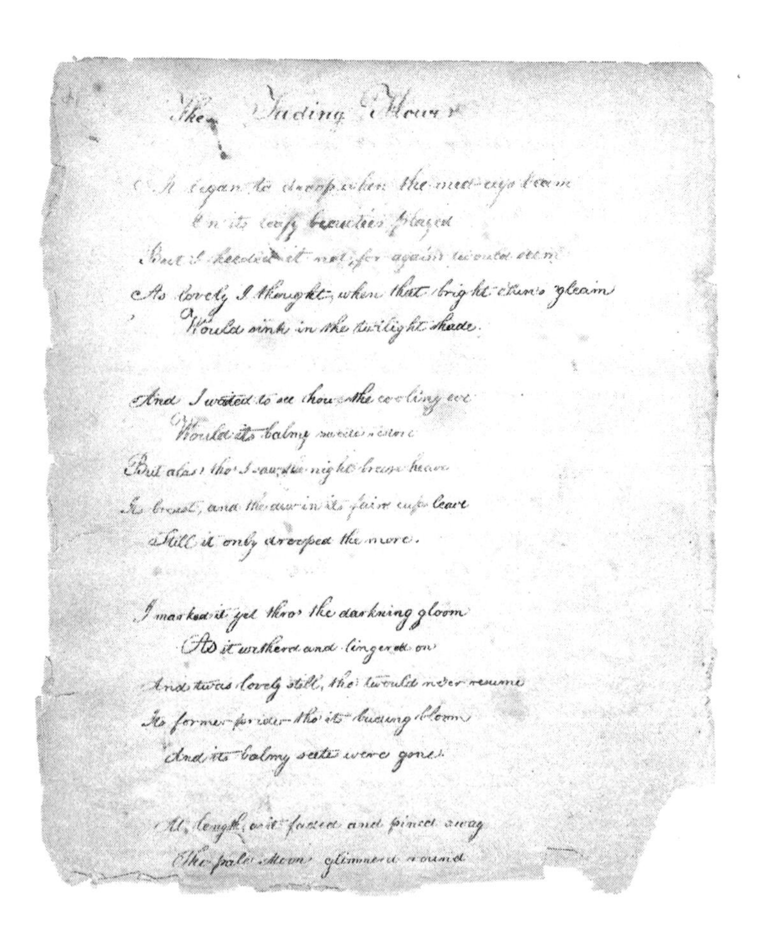

The Fading Flower

It began to droop when the mid-day beam
On its leafy beauties played
But I heeded it not, for again would seem
As lovely I thought, when that bright sun's gleam
Would sink in the twilight shade.

And I waited to see how the cooling eve
Would its balmy sweets restore
But alas! tho' I saw the night breeze heave
Its breast, and the dew in its fair cup leave
Still it only drooped the more.

I marked it yet thro' the darkning gloom
As it withered and lingered on
And twas lovely still, tho' it would never resume
Its former pride— tho' its budding bloom
And its balmy sweets were gone.

At length, as it faded and pined away
The pale Moon glimmered round

From *The Fading Flower,* by O.J. Honre, page 26

3d When I was in the field a hoeing
Near the set of sun
Glad to hear the horn a blowin
To tell that the work was done
From the darkey's frolick sweetly
Banjo in tune
Dine and Tillie dressed so neatly
Danced by the big round moon

4th One little hut among the bushes
One whoom I do love
Still fondly to my memory rushes
No mater where I rove
When will I hear the bees a humming
All among the comb
When will I hear the Banjo tuning
Down in my good old home
Chorus All the world seems sad and dreary
Every where I roam
Oh, Brothers how my heart grows weary
Far from the old folks at home
L.B.x.

From *The Old Folks at Home*, inscribed by Martha Light, page 111

Within this hallowed shrine;
To think that o'er these lines thine eye
May wander in some future year,
And Memory breathe a passing sigh
For her who traced them here.
Calm sleeps the sea when storms are o'er,
With bosom silent and serene,
And but the plank upon the shore
Reveals that wrecks have been;
So some frail leaf like this may be
Left floating on Time's silent tide,
The sole remaining trace of me,
To tell I lived and died.

Athens Oct. 28, th 1831 P. A. M.

One of five poems by Ann Maxon, page 43

Supplement

GUIDELINES TO START AND KEEP AN ALBUM LIKE HARRIET'S

The poems on these pages show how one can use an easy-to-learn format to create something quite amazing. Regular, ordinary folks created this beautiful and charming document; a document full of meaning in the Light family.

And what family would not want a similar document? Who wouldn't want a hundred years of family history chronicled in poetry? The contributors to Harriet's album teach the power of even academically undistinguished poems to chronicle and reveal, when one sees what a beautiful portrait had been painted of her in the words of not just one person but of many people. This portrait is as clear as any photograph and twice as revealing. Of all the historical documents reviewed researching this work nothing was more personally revealing than the poems themselves.

This technique can work for anyone. Poetically-challenged people can do this and gifted poets should also. All one needs is passion and a muse like Harriet.

Thanks to these poetic poltergeists, we today can follow their guidelines and create an album for our own families, one that may be passed down and cherished by generations to come. Along the way is the added benefit of also passing down an appreciation for poetry in general by having a body of work built into your family with deep meaning and significance.

Perhaps Harriet's album is not so much a book as it is a quilt, not of fabric but of words, stitched together by seventy people over eighty years. Each poem is a single square of the quilt. Begin the stitching for your own poetic family quilt, then, set it off upon its own journey through life.

1. Start the album as a group of close friends and family. Beginning the work as a group, in and of itself is very poignant, moreover it will set the standard of the book.

Future contributors are more likely to adhere to those standards when they see how well it was begun. The purpose of the album need not be a poetic intervention, as was the case with Harriet's, it could just as easily be created purely in celebration. Adapt it to your unique conditions.

2. The group writes original poems or finds a poem by another. Either way the poems are for, about and dedicated to whoever will be the recipient of the album. Whether original or borrowed your poem should be a message from you to the album recipient so themes like remembrance, forget-me-not, friendship, hopes and dreams are very appropriate as well as apothegms (see below).
3. The poems or entries are to be handwritten in the album by each person in ink, having been completed and checked for completeness in advance. The finished work should be as mistake-free as possible so the album is also pleasing to see. Renaissance commonplace books often had a "master-reader" to lead the group so you may want to find a local, talented wordsmith to help out, as AG Brown helped Harriet's friends. The handwritten part is important also for the benefit of future readers or users of your album. You can tell much about someone from their handwriting. Harriet's album, with it's seventy contributor's many styles of writing, has the feel of a rich and varied tapestry. The printed word is efficient but the handwritten word is intimate and revealing.
4. Limit your journalistic entries! The only journalistic part of your entry should be signing, dating and saying where the poem was written (which is important, it will greatly aid future generations to figure out the story behind the poems and where the album might have ventured in its life). Good quotes, sayings and lyrics should be the main contributions, other than poems if you want to achieve a feel, similar to Harriet's, in your own album.

5. Time-honored truths or apothegms are also important. A commonplace book is traditionally a reference book, a single vessel which collects those many kernels of knowledge and wisdom, in the form of quotes, poems and sayings, which are important to us. Being time-honored, it is likely these truths will continue to have meaning for future generations. One of the things that kept Harriet's album active for so long was that the poets passed down their values and beliefs, not just random poems. Subsequent owners, like Martha Ann related to those very sentiments and values and it helped keep the book alive.
6. The owner or recipient of the album should, for the most part, let others fill the pages of the album. Harriet wrote only two poems in her album. The album should be an intimate, tangible reminder of friends and family over the years, a place to visit with them even if separated by great time or distance. Harriet's album was a tremendous comfort to her in tough times and there is no reason to believe it won't be the same with your album.
7. Pass the book down. Ensure that it continues to be used by involving your friends and family with it. Share it, use it, read the poems aloud. Encourage people to think about what piece they want to write in the album. Make them a part of it so they will be comfortable and familiar with it. If they are already involved, when the time comes to pass it on they will know what to do to keep the story going and, moreover, will have the desire to do so.

"Where ere you go, where ere you rove,
may happiness be your lot."

Index of Poems

LaVergne, TN USA
02 March 2011
218457LV00004B/3/P

9 781609 100339